KNOCK AND WAIT

ARNOLD F WARD

SANDBOX PUBLICATIONS

In loving memory of my dear mother, Verona

*"He would rest beneath the tree and remember,
his heart sad with loss yet filled with wonder and
gratitude. He would cradle there in its shelter
and support, his mind sucking strength from her
ever-living spirit and her never-dying love."*

SMOODY'S STORY

Send down another tendril

Let it
Strike
and Grow
Strong BAOBAB
draw your children to yourself as one
Show us the WAY.

They say that the gift of memory; the ability to record and recall, was given to us so that we could treasure the good things, savour the joys and beauties of Life. Why then, Smoody thought, do we always seem to dwell upon the pain we experienced, and caused? Why do negative memories stand out more sharply than happy recollections?

He was no different, he knew. For whenever he would read it .. the Poem .. He would think of Sam. Not brilliant, young Samuel Spencer, schoolteacher and poet. Not "Sweetmout' Sam" the man with all the girls... But drunken, pissy Sam, who left his mother's nice wall bungalow to live in "the Jungle" and sleep in the bus stand.

The poem would remind him of pleasant times. The teenage hours he spent as a member of his church group. The friendship, the fun; the outings in the country; the sense of purpose and accomplishment; whether at dominoes, debating or volleyball. He relished the memory of evenings at the Rooftop Cafe guzzling too sweet milkshakes and eating greasy hamburgers. It was a beautiful spot. One side of the building afforded a view of the cars and other traffic hustling along the narrow road that tried to pass itself off as a highway. The other side overlooked the bay: placid and deep blue enhanced at twilight with shades of shimmering brass and gold.

Often, very often, his mind would recall and ponder these things, but, inevitably, his thoughts would return to Sam. Sam, who, perhaps in search of new adventures and experiences, or maybe, in an attempt to make some tragic liberal statement – Sam, bearing the burden of the whole world on his puny shoulders, had left the group. He had tried to assimilate the mores and manners of the gamblers, drunkards and prostitutes who infested his new home. But he was a middle class boy .. a salt water fish in a polluted pond. Nobody was surprised when they found him one day ... Dead! Lying in an alley that smelled like the inside of an old outhouse. Some animal had taken all his money, then dropped something on him. Something heavy enough to crush his brilliant skull.

His new rummy friends disrupted the funeral. They poured liquor on the casket and swore at each other throughout the service. People were annoyed but their lack of respect did not appear to upset the pastor. His bearing, as usual, was noble. His delivery eloquent. His soft eyes surveyed these rebels with a sadness, a passion, an understanding that they could not fathom and his great soul embraced them through the sounds that issued from his lips.

"The Love we feel and share too often brings us here, to this .. Tragedy. Sometimes it brings us cruel words of separation; often to death and futile tears. BUT LOVE, CHILDREN. LOVE! Remember: 'Though I speak with the tongues of men and of Angels and have not love I am become as sounding brass or a tinkling cymbal.' Sometime, children, in your debates, in your youthful thirst for enlightenment, you question the very existence of God. I say, Religion is based on faith and so is our very existence from day to day. Breathe in that vital, invisible, air believing that it will always be there. Rejoice in the light manifested by the electric current flowing into your lamp. You do not see it but you perceive and enjoy the result. You sometimes question the senselessness of poverty and pain. The perversion, the utter waste of youth, beauty and intelligence that today we are gathered here to mourn. I sigh and tell you HOPE. Strive children, and hope. Remember most of all, my friends, brethren and children.."

His dark eyes would burn, his voice boom like thunder in our ears.

"LOVE ONE ANOTHER! Love your mother when she scolds you, Love your sister when she teases

you. Forget the petty jealousies and competitive-
ness of youth. Love your enemies in spite of their
actions. Love them for their Humanity. Remember GOD is Love and

LOVE IS GOD!"

He clasped his hands. He looked toward heaven.

"Show us the way"

Behold this silk strand
Bullied by Wind
Grow stiff to
Pierce the bruised Earth
sucking her
Strength
Show us the WAY

Smoody was glad when the offer of the scholarship to study overseas came along. He had seen other graduates return home to take up important sounding jobs and make good money. The idea of leaving home to live alone did not frighten him. He had seen "TO SIR, WITH LOVE" and yearned romantically for the freedom of his own little flat; cooking his own meals, doing his own laundry, entertaining friends. It all seemed like an exciting adventure to him.

But there was much more than he could have imagined. The first two years at university were the longest and perhaps the most significant of his entire life. He had to view so many images, bury so many myths and misconceptions. It was an awakening, an exhilarating introduction to the beauty, the sheer joy of reasoning, analysing, accepting and rejecting ideas. He could argue with and criticise the actions of the current power brokers. He was the product of a deferential society he had been trained to hero-worship Presidents and Prime Ministers; Kings and Queens. He now perceived them as fallible and foolish tyrants, racists .... human .. and often because of the "power" they were allowed to wield ... inhuman.

Unfortunately, he also discovered within himself a devastating wit. He had always been a jovial sort of fellow, the product of a happy childhood. Now, it seemed, the clever twists and puns, the mild sarcasm, were replaced with cruelty and arrogance. His tongue, they said, was sharp. In discussion or debate he could verbally cripple an opponent. Maybe it was because he was lonely and unhappy. He missed home. He had no friends and he had begun to forget how to make them. He had been accustomed to meeting with his youth group every evening to enjoy cricket, dominoes and other games. There would always be laughter, talk of past and upcoming activities and although not specifically recognised, a great deal of emotional and psychological support. Now each of his few acquaintances, students like himself, lived at least ten miles away and he would see them once a month .. at most. They had jobs and were always busy. He was not allowed to work. Nor could he make friends with the other tenants in his dingy rooming house. They were all women, older women, women with moustaches, paunches and vicious looking boyfriends. There was no lock on his bedroom door and these "ladies" were not attractive enough to die for.

He was suffering. The big city is a place where no stranger looks you in the eye. No one touches you without a hasty and impersonal apology. Yet here, paradoxically, sex is king. It overshadows everything and everyone. Every word, every song can be a sexual inducement. Every edifice a phallic symbol. Every member of every race, every woman, every man ... God help us .. every child .. is clothed, fed, befriended, evaluated according to his/her "sex appeal". For others it seemed so easy to adapt but Smoody found it difficult to "get with" all that was going on. He sensed that they considered him desirable; the white girls with their bold looks, tight smiles and patronising conversation; the black "sisters" with their over-hip talk and provocative dances. And he could feel his senses, his needs, urging him on. He was twenty years old, and, although he did not recognise it himself he was literally being driven crazy by submerged and suppressed desires. He was forced, partly by economic constraints, partly by his changing mental state, to consciously deny himself the things he most needed.

When Agatha invited him to her flat for lunch he sensed that the menu she planned went far beyond the curried chicken and rice he could smell cooking. He would have welcomed this; it would have helped to ease the tension he always felt. Besides, he loved her, in a platonic way. He could not imagine himself being intimate with a person that he did not at least like. He loved her for her intelligence for she was not beautiful. Her most pleasing features were her well-formed oval face and her large, expressive eyes. She was running to fat. She would argue that she was "pleasingly plump" and at this early stage her plumpness caused her dark skin to appear soft and silky. Her hair was closely cropped, like a boy's, yet she seemed entirely feminine without affectation. She was widely read and could snap off references, facts and figures at will to dazzle and defeat those foolish enough to cross mental swords with her. Her expressive hands cut the air. Her large eyes beamed fierce conviction as she battled another battle in her endless crusade to enfranchise women and minorities.

But she was a lousy cook. The rice was unbelievably hard. "Like bullets" his mother would say. The chicken was too salt and there was too much pepper in the curry. He ate no more than a few spoonfuls. He was not one to inconvenience himself in order to spare the feelings of others. He pushed the plate away and got up to leave the table.

"May I use the washroom?"

"No, fool." She joked. Then .. "It's through the bedroom and to your left."

When he came out of the bathroom she was

there...in the bedroom. Pointedly making the bed. He looked at her for a moment. He wondered what would happen if he tried to embrace her. He imagined her melting, as they say, in his arms. Then the fear of rejection overcame him. He looked at her again. She pretended not to notice him but bent over to smooth the sheets. The soft curvature of her buttocks was innocently blocking his exit. He almost panicked. "Excuse me." He managed in a hoarse whisper as he brushed swiftly by her and made his way into the living room.

She came and placed a scotch and soda on the table for him then mixed a Bloody Mary for herself.

"You are as kind as you are beautiful." He said.

"Y'know," she said, lighting a cigarette. "I am beginning to agree with Vincent. You're an okay guy beneath all that aggressiveness."

Aggressiveness? What the hell was she talking about?
"Seen through me, eh?" He parried with a weak smile.

"You can also be obsequious as hell."

This broad was going too far. If she kept this up it would be a very short conversation. He went over to the couch. "Shall I lie down, Doctor?" He sprawled out casually.

Her eyes surveyed the muscular chest, gazed at the deep cavity where the abdomen was stretched into a taut depression by the knotty arms used to pillow his head. She licked her lips.

"As you please." She tried to sound flippant. She took a quick sip from her Bloody Mary and continued. "You're a nice boy, Smoody. A nice looking, very good looking, boy but you seem to lack respect for people."

He opened his mouth to say something then decided against it. Let her talk. She would stop when she ran out of words. He closed his eyes to indicate a lack of interest in the conversation.

She was not so easily deterred. "I think that this aggressive, aloof attitude you display is a defence mechanism. I believe the culture shock of your moving from the islands to the big city has affected you in this way. You get defensive. You set up a barrier. You try to project a strong, self-sufficient, unconcerned image and you lash out and say terrible, hurting things to people because you are afraid."

"Why?" He asked. "What is there to be afraid of?"

"Rejection." She took another sip from her drink. "It is everywhere, and everyone is afraid of it."

How well he knew rejection. It had been first to greet him as his plane landed at the airport and now accompanied him every day through the streets. It occupied the empty seat next to him on the bus, the subway and in the cinemas. It was an unwelcome companion whose depressing influence he always sought to avoid.

"In the big city", she continued, "no one trusts strangers. There is little that is spontaneous in human relationships. Everything.. even 'making love' here she formed quotation marks with her fingers.... "is impersonal. I get your name from a computer or some tasteless ad in the newspaper. Or I meet you at a party, screw you and never even bother to ask your name. People here are busy. They are concerned with their individual problems, with their own little worlds."
She knocked the ash from her cigarette, took a long draw and continued. "In the islands there is spontaneity. Strangers shout your name as you walk down the street. Here, you don't know the name of your next door neighbour. Back home you belong to a green world, a living world. You hear the sound of fowl-cocks crowing every morning. You enjoy the shouts of children playing while on their way to school. When you hear loud music in the night you rush out to join in the revelry. Here you spend months in a heavy coat imprisoned in a dingy, airless room. Instead of dogs and fowl-cocks you hear police sirens rushing to put out the loud music at some party."

He sat up. the peace. Sounds of life disturbed

the peace. He often yearned to find some desolate place where he could shout and shout and shout.

"So how come it doesn't affect you?"

"Oh, it affects everybody but in different ways. I'm luckier than most. I have relatives here. They looked after me when I first came. Showed me the ropes. I'm a lot of woman in case you haven't noticed. I never get lonely."

Sure. She would not get lonely. What with Vincent and Chiggaboom and Mugsy always running behind her. He could see it now. He was too aloof. He presented a challenge to her. She had to conquer him. Women, it seemed, needed to believe themselves to be irresistible.

She came over and sat down on the couch beside him. She bent over slowly to place her bloody Mary on the centre table.

"Smoody." She was saying. "If you continue like this you are going to end up bitter and cold. You will have destroyed what I am sure used to be a truly beautiful personality. Reach out, Smoody. Reach out and get help before it's too late!" He noticed with a start that the back of her dress was opened to the waist. Her skin gleamed dully in the soft light. He could see no bra straps. There was nothing under that flimsy thing!

"TOUCH IT!" His mind screamed. "Run your hands over it, you fool! She wants you to touch it."

Slowly, clumsily, he reached up. His trembling left hand hovered over her back. He realised that he could not reach it. He had to get closer. He shifted his body nervously, stretched out and .. knocked over the centre table! Their glasses crashed and crumpled on the floor, the Bloody Mary becoming a huge, red blush on the white shag carpet. He sprang up! He felt an inadequate fool. He was changing. Something terrible was happening to his mind. He could not face her. He had to leave ... *He just had to get out that door*!

Even before he left home he had been looking forward to his return. During the first two years of his sojourn overseas, his consciousness would return home every night as he slept and he would awaken each morning with a start, surprised at not being in his own bed with his little brother beside him.

At first he imagined himself arriving proudly at the airport, showing off his diploma to his friends. There would be the inevitable party afterwards, he was sure. Once again, at last, he would enjoy that sense of identity; that feeling of belonging that he seemed to have lost. Soon, very soon, he would be able to safely shed the heavy armour he had developed to counter years of subtle, and blatant, attacks on his self-esteem.

But change, although certain, is often indiscernible, and after some time his return home receded further in his mind until it became almost a thing of insignificance.

As his workload at college increased he became more and more isolated, physically and emotionally. He would often spend the long winter days in his room with arguments and counter arguments, ideas of all description, some cynical, some amusing, some weird, passing through his mind. Although he perceived that he was at the zenith of his mental development he also realised that his spirit had been sapped of all vitality. His angry and horrified preoccupation with the past and present suffering of humanity had stolen all the joy from his once vibrant soul. He pondered the frustration, the apparent disorder into which the world had thrown itself. Prejudice and greed he identified as the causes and his mind constantly searched for a remedy.

He wondered about God. Why would a benevolent, all-powerful being allow such chaos to continue for so long when he, a frail human had managed to devise a solution? If he had the power; If he could conceive the means, he would force each aggressor to experience the suffering he was inflicting. Let slave masters, he thought, feel the sting of the whip. Let murderers suffer the sharp pain as the knife tears skin and flesh, the complete havoc as bullets make their way through the skull. Let tyrants know the helplessness of children with distended bellies; feel their frustration as flies play and defecate on their unwashed faces. If every man responsible for every robbery, rape, theft or murder, he reasoned. If every man who ever lied or slandered or humiliated another could be made to share the suffering of his victim, then the world's problems would be swiftly and completely eliminated.   From this new, godlike vantage point he therefore viewed the transportation of his body from one point on the globe to another with indifference. He had grown to hate a fuss. So he completed his examinations and without waiting for the graduation ceremony, without even informing his family, boarded a plane to the island.

It was night when he arrived. He passed through Customs and quickly hired a taxi. He found the now unfamiliar darkness to be overpoweringly seductive and the noises coming from the swaying cane fields they passed hinted at mysterious and tantalising goings on. He also found himself dodging involuntarily as they near-missed people walking complacently on the wrong side of the street. They passed a rundown two door shop. "PORGY'S PINK PALACE!" The sign informed them.

"Buck Rogers! Buck Rogers!" A voice called from somewhere.

"Aieee!" His driver shouted back.

"Man stop a minute, nuh."

"Comin' back!" His driver shouted and

started to drive a little faster. "Dominoes." He muttered. "And rum. That is all they know."

◆ ◆ ◆

His mother hugged him. And hugged him. His younger relatives gaped at him. Everybody else questioned him until he became bored and edgy. Then, they let him go to bed.

Next morning he walked down to the beach. The low buildings and narrow streets made him feel tall and at the same time strangely insecure. He could not help noticing how small and dingy everything appeared. Here and there a broken guard wall would reveal a disorderly tangle of dry grass and scraggly vine covered trees.

He reached the beach. It too seemed much smaller than he had remembered. He stepped eagerly on the bleached sand feeling it warm and yielding beneath his feet. The ocean waved a foamy blue and white hand at him. The air, fresh and raw, struck and swirled about his hot body. He closed his eyes, sucked in a lungful, exhaled and sucked in another. For the first time, his omnipresent tension seemed to ease a little. He started to remember now, his days as KARNAK THE CONQUEROR, how he would brace his twelve year old body in the water, repelling attack after attack from Charlie, John-John and ... Sam. Here. On this very beach, the terrible Karnak had fought and won several water battles and wrestling matches. Valiantly had he

"Smoody!? Man I ain't know you in the islun' ?"

"Hey! Smoooody! Say something, Spar."

They were seated under the casuarinas shouting and waving to him. He went over, smiling. They shook him by the hand, patted his back; voiced loudly and with enthusiasm their joy at having him back. He tried desperately to shake off his reserve but it was useless. As they questioned him he soon became bored and angry at the materialistic misinformation they had been fed about the big city. To them he had been to Utopia and back. They wanted to hear about high-rise apartments with saunas and swimming pools not furnished rooms with soiled beds and cockroaches. They wanted large, air-conditioned cars not freezing bus stops and draughty subway terminals. Unfortunately, he had of late developed an evangelical desire to enlighten every and anyone who would listen to him. To share the knowledge he had so suffered to acquire. If education and empathy were to save the world he was more than prepared to play a large part in its salvation. And so he stated his facts from a position of authority and would brook no contradiction. He quieted his questioners with his devastating wit, cutting deep into their veneer of knowledge and exposing their naiveté and ignorance. The scars from past put-downs and humiliations he callously re-opened and displayed until one by one they mumbled excuses and rushed off to hide themselves in the water leaving him lonely and victorious on the sand.

◆ ◆ ◆

From that time onward he committed one social gaffe after another. He was surprised to find that his every action, his most innocent statement would later become the subject of local discussion and debate. In the big city he had been one of three million nameless statistics. Here every one seemed to know him personally and had apparently decided to place him under their collective microscope. He, on the other hand, paid them absolutely no attention. His mind was always busy, always taken up with profound thoughts. Very often he did not even see or hear the people around him and would pass by them without offering the expected smile and greeting. His old friends and neighbours, the simple people who had seen him struggle and grow, who had encouraged and assisted him, now thought him a proud, arrogant, ungrateful young man.

It was no better at the office. He had acquired work at a bank, an institution then infested with a particularly crotchety variety of spinster. Robbed of their social potential, the love of a husband and children, by the demands of the job, these once beautiful and desirable women slowly developed into cruel and bitter shells, never slow to vent their nervous tension on their unfortunate subordinates.

Miss McGraw was typical. She disliked him intensely and nagged him unmercifully. He was too bright, too quick to grasp and perform the work. She hated his attitude. He lacked respect. For some reason he never accorded her the deference she was accustomed to receiving from people like him. He seemed to want to treat her as an equal! He was uppity. That's what he was .. Uppity! And so she decided that she would have him fired if it was the last thing she ever did.

As it turned out it was not a difficult thing to do. Smoody did not care much for the job. It was routine and dull. The hours were rotten and the constant whining of those dried up old broads was a colossal pain. It happened one Friday afternoon. The bank was busy. Smoody was pooped and Miss McGraw had been racked for hours by one of her migraines. It was four-thirty when she rushed up to his desk.

"Mr. Blackman. Look at this Cash Book. It's a mess ... and full of mistakes."

She was calling him incompetent in front of the Accountant. Right in front of all the customers she was accusing him of errors he had not made. That was not his Cash Book in her hand. Something snapped. Some of the rage he had been concealing for so long broke its constraints and spilled all over her. He told her several things. Things calculated to wound, humiliate even terrify her. He used cuss-words no one had heard for a long time and never in the bank. Then, amid shocked silence, he snatched up his briefcase and walked unconcernedly outside.

The midday sun outside of the old fashioned building was brilliant. He felt a surge of relief. A sense of release from the tension, the backbiting, yes .. the hate that had filled the atmosphere in that place. His steps took him to the rooftop cafe. He had not been there since his return. It looked the same to him as before. Things in his homeland changed slowly, almost imperceptibly.

He ordered a milkshake and when it arrived, in a large, goblet-like glass with a saucer and a paper napkin, it tasted exactly like the hundreds he had consumed before with his friends. In the old days when he used to have friends. His new, aloof attitude had made it impossible for him to make friends nowadays. He had many acquaintances but nobody close. No confidantes. He was now an object. A curiosity to observe and discuss. He felt overcome with hurt, frustration and anger.

They had warned him that it would be difficult to fit back in ... those he had met before who had found it necessary to exile themselves in order to preserve their sanity. He could now relate to their distress. Like them he was too good, too enlightened for this narrow-minded little island. But exile was not the solution. He disliked plastic people even more than pretentious small islanders.

He picked up his napkin and wiped his mouth. He looked at the rumpled ball in his hand. There was something written in the corner.

"Judge not and ye shall not be judged: condemn not and ye shall not be condemned, forgive and ye shall be forgiven." Luke 6:37

He looked at it for a while, weighing and considering every word. If the "Rev" were here he would probably quote those exact words. Perhaps he would use another of his favourites. The one he always used when he found youngsters fussing or about to fight.

"For if ye forgive men their trespasses your Heavenly Father will also forgive you."

He felt so ashamed. He had let everyone down. His mother; his schoolteachers, the lecturers at college and especially the "Rev" who had spent so much time counselling him; who had made no secret of the trust he had invested in him. A tear escaped from his right eye. He dabbed at it quickly, hoping that no one had noticed.

"Things will not always be easy, my boy."

The voice, soft and eerie, seemed to be right next to his ear. It could have been the 'Rev's' voice but it also sounded like Sam's. Smoody shivered.

"You are special. You are strong. Shine, Smoody, Shine. `Let not thy heart be troubled neither let it be afraid.... Seek righteousness, Son. Sow seeds of Love.'"

A gust of wind snatched the napkin from his hand. He watched it as it dipped and fluttered, like a small white cloud, over the car park. Then, once over the bay, it began to rise. He watched it, still rising, become a speck in the distance and knew, in his heart, that it would never fall to the ground.

The morning after when past joy begets insecurity when freedom fathers fear. His body forced him to rise at the usual six-thirty. He started the rush to the bathroom to prepare himself for work. Then his mind wrestled itself back to reality. There was no reason to hurry. He was free, now. Or was he? For he was alive and he had needs. As long as there was need, physical and emotional need, there could be no freedom.

A stab of fear. An unfamiliar dread now gripped his soul. What was it that he feared? Not the loss of some of his freedom. No one could expect to be totally free. He knew that and was therefore not unwilling to make some sacrifice. All he wanted was to reserve the right to be himself.

What was it then, that he feared? No. He did not fear the questions, comments and vicious speculation of his neighbours and the so-called friends of his family nor was he concerned that there would be hurt or despair in his mother's eyes. She loved him and the more he blundered the greater would be her love. Her support. He could continue until his dying day to ignore her soft admonitions and be met only with tender understanding. She knew him well. She had met him long before in the blunt tongue of the otherwise warm and generous Granny Blackman and in the fearless features of 'Big Boy' Blackman, legendary lighter man and amateur boxer - his father. She was prepared to trust and guide him as much as she could relying on the grace of God to guarantee an eventual positive outcome.

What then did he fear? Perhaps he feared himself. His capacity to "mess up himself", as Kelly at college always used to say. What was it about him? Other people seemed to manage their lives so easily yet he would always find it difficult to accomplish anything. Even the simple desire to peacefully coexist with those around him seemed impossible to attain. There seemed to be no peace for him. What was it about him? How was he different? Why did he so often tend to attract the attentions of negative forces?

He thrust these thoughts from his mind. His first priority was to get another job. His meagre savings would not last forever. He decided to submit his resume to a number of the best firms in the city. There was a dearth of talented and educated people in the country it would not be long, he thought, before some company snapped him up.

But months passed and he received no replies to his letters of application., not even acknowledgement of his correspondence. He was surprised but not worried. He had to be patient, he thought. All good things took time. He was prepared to wait until the very best opportunity came along.

Besides, he was enjoying this enforced vacation. He spent long hours at the beach, rediscovering and revitalising his strong, young body. Then at dusk he would visit the village rum shop, have a beer or two and play dominoes with the fishermen, the gardeners and artisans who congregated there. He was slowly beginning to re-integrate himself into the village life. He was beginning to remember and respond to the little courtesies, the humour, and the insults - the nuances that formed the character of the community of which he was once more beginning to believe himself to be a part.

One evening somebody asked: "Smoody, you find work yet?"

He was aware that they discussed him behind his back. Now it seemed that the curiosity about his situation and his future plans had probably become too much for them and somebody had volunteered to bell the cat.

"Not yet." He said. Strange. He had not thought about his job situation for some time.

"A man like you shouldn't have no trouble finding work. I hear you got a lot of certificates."

"Certificates ain't all." Somebody else said. "You does got to have a godfather, too."

"It take very long for you to get a job. You must be 'pon somebody black list."

"Well I black, you know." Smoody offered weakly. He was beginning to become uncomfortable. He wished the conversation would end.

"I know a fellow who couldn't get a job 'bout here at all." The first speaker continued. "One of the big boys say that he was never to work in this island again and nobody at all won't hire he."

Smoody found it hard to understand the devilish mentality that would deny another human being the natural right to employment. " God gave you two hands to work for yourself and a brain to think for yourself." But tin gods would bind those hands and stifle the talent in that brain, suffocating and murdering the victim and his innocent dependents. Why?

The others in the rum shop continued to discuss the several cases of petty victimisation they had heard, read about, or experienced. Smoody was silent. The more he thought about his situation the more he began to realise that something was indeed wrong. He decided to investigate the matter.

Next morning he called the bank.

"Miss McGraw speaking."

He placed a handkerchief over the mouthpiece and assumed his best North American accent.

"Good morning, Miss McGraw. I'm calling here from Odette Industries. We plan to open a plant in your island next month. We advertised for an Office Manager and are now screening the applicants. Do you know a Mr. Black..."

She did not even wait for him to finish the question before she launched into a practised and well-worn character assassination routine. It was everything a prospective employer did not want to hear. Only a madman would hire the creature she fabricated. Smoody was hurt, disappointed and surprised to hear himself so unfairly misrepresented. He had a lot to learn about human nature. He tended to credit others with too much nobility.

"Aw .. come on. He can't be that bad." He said during a break in the litany. But he had been distracted by the abuse. A hint of his island accent came through.

"Who is this?" Miss McGraw asked, startled.

Smoody did not answer.

"Who is this?" Miss McGraw almost shrieked.

"Smoody decided to frighten her some more. "You goin' soon find out." He said in the roughest voice he could muster, and hung up the phone.

◆ ◆ ◆

The pain, surprise and hurt soon gave way to anger. An anger which now introduced him to the wild creature that lived and raged within him. To an uncontrollable madness in his breast, tearing his heart with fury, burning his bowels with passionate indignation. His soul was almost ready to accept and implement the many ways that this beast devised for him to avenge himself. He could do it. He could execute every one of these destructive suggestions. He had the strength and the intellect to wreak the havoc this monster was suggesting. Right was on his side. Justice would be done. He would be a hero here, a villain there, but he would be avenged.

Yet ... something stayed his hand, something in his upbringing. Perhaps it was the love for his mother and family. Perhaps it was the re-awakening of the awareness of himself as a member of the village community. He owed these people. He was still a symbol, though slightly tarnished, of their pride. He could not let them down. He had to somehow manage to overcome the present situation; to raise himself from this pile of rubbish and shine.

But the injustice of it kept gnawing at him. The brooding recollection kept wearing him down. "Hey, Smoody. You drinking very strong!" they would remark at first but soon became accustomed to seeing him every evening empty a pint'n'a half bottle. Later he became a regular sight staggering unaware through the village. Unaware of who and where he was. Unaware, even of his mother's failing health. Absent when she, also lacking the will to live, decided to take her leave.

He did not attend the funeral. He spent that time on the rocks overlooking the bay. One part of his mind fought to imagine the activities at the church and at the graveside while he struggled unsuccessfully to steer it in other directions. He should have been there. The first son should have been there. He should not have been denied the right to purchase the finest casket, the biggest wreaths, the prettiest hymn sheets with the sweetest hymns.

He sighed and sucked his teeth. What could he do? It was the work of his invisible tormentors. It was their fault. But the thought persisted. He should be there, ensuring that everything went smoothly. Did they take that photo from her dresser and place it in her arms? The picture of his father in uniform, marching off to die in World War Two. 'Massa Bassa Bassa' as he called it. Shame took hold of him; grief once more flooded his soul. He pulled the flask from his back pocket and sucked in desperation.

A group of children were fishing on the rocks near him, clambering over the sharp edges with their roughened bare feet. Baiting and tossing their lines. Arguing and cursing. They had greeted him as he arrived with shouts of derisive laughter. They liked to point at him, laugh and call him the Drunken Professor. They had imitated the way he stumbled along nudging each other and chortling in glee. He paid them no attention. He was no stranger to ridicule and abuse.

He remembered the day he dirtied his pants on his way home from school. He recalled how his little friends kept a safe distance from him as they joked and jeered his every step home. Then they ran away, subjecting him to the more tender mercies of the 'big people'- big in body, small in mind. They would not let this opportunity to shame him pass them by. The weak and unfortunate were placed on this earth to be humiliated. Those persons beside the road laughing and crudely gesticulating were living testimony to this fact of life. They took their daily licks and passed them on. Smoody wanted to run from their reproach, to hide and cry. But he walked quietly on. Something in his small soul forced him to confront this new adversity and stare it squarely in the eye. And so he walked on. Past the stares and comments, past the tasteless jokes. Only as he neared home did his little shoulders start to ache with shame and fear for he could see his mother waiting outside for him. Was that anger or anxiety that clouded her face? Would he be scolded and flogged? Perhaps this was the time for him to run. Run, run, run and never return. Still his weary feet persisted. Pressing on to the place where she stood, waiting to reach gently down to lift and hug his shitty little body. At last he knew that it was safe for him to cry.

Now she was gone and he was left hurt and handicapped on this hard cliff top. He wished that he, too, could die. A tear tried to force itself from his dry and burning eyes. He closed them but this caused his liquor filled head to spin. A few moments rest. *A little rest...* He lay back on the jagged surface. Maybe when he awoke something would have changed.

But the damn children were shouting again. Screaming at the top of their shrill little voices. Why the hell did they have to carry on like that? They had no manners. He once more experienced a powerful, all consuming anger. He would deal with them. Let him find a piece of stick and he would make them sorry. He forced his eyes open to try to determine the cause of the commotion and realised that one of the children, a young boy had fallen from the rocks. Smoody could see him thrashing about helplessly in the water below. *"Dead you noisy little rat!"* Smoody thought. *"Dead quick and let the rest of them keep quiet!"* He watched with satisfaction as the struggling figure disappeared under the waves but after a moment it reappeared, a little further from the shore.

"Save me! Somebody help me!" Smoody, still looking, was amazed at what he saw. There were now two figures bobbing in the dip and swell of the waves. The splashing figure of the boy and a new presence – a beautiful lady clothed in a white gown. His mother, her youthful complexion skilfully simulated by pink powder, her sunken cheeks replenished with cotton wool. He could see her now ride the water keeping the boy afloat. The voice he heard above the cacophony of shouts and screams emanating from the other children was hers, filled with pain and alarm. *"Save my son! ..Please save my son!"*

"Mama!" Smoody rushed over the rocks and dived into the sea below. Blindly, clumsily. The liquor in his head affected his judgement and he dived too soon. His left shoulder crashed into the jagged edge of a boulder as he fell. He felt a sharp pain and then his arm went numb. Mercifully, the shock of the force with which he struck the water combined with its cold welcome to partly open the chemical prison encircling his mind. He was a strong swimmer; he was a determined man when motivated. There was nothing on earth that could prevent him from reaching that boy and transporting him, gulping and gasping to the

shore.

◆ ◆ ◆

My change!" Congo said.

Nobody answered.

"I say I want my change. I had four iron dollars in my pocket just now. They not there now. I want them!"

Congo was drunk and angry tonight. It was not wise to deal with him in this mood. Not long ago he had staggered into the rum shop and everybody hurriedly sized round as he sprawled his huge body on the bench by the draughts and domino table. Nobody greeted him. He was vexed tonight and should be left alone. Tonight was not the night to steal his money with cards and dominoes. When a woman caught him with his head "sweet" she could fool him, promising delights he would soon be unable to enjoy. But tonight was not the night for he was drunk, really drunk. Drunk and angry. He was a man to avoid. So everybody watched with concealed fury as, without invitation he proceeded to empty their bottle of white rum. Then they watched with fearful amusement as his big, knotty head slowly lowered itself to the tabletop and a trickle of translucent slime began to issue from between his teeth. Several loud snores and the massive frame started to slide from the table and ease towards the floor. It was then that the four coins made their shy appearance. As Congo's body slipped from the bench they dribbled from a side pocket to tinkle invitingly onto the floor. Nobody saw the hand that retrieved them but everybody enjoyed the rum and smoked the cigarettes that they had helped to procure.

"My change!" Congo now insisted. "I ain' leavin' this place until I see my money. Even if I got to beat every so an' so body in here. Even if I got to go up to prison again."

"Why are weaklings so noisy?" Poodle was a short, skinny, 'red' man. His voice a high-pitched sneer. *"Why do brutes possess so little courage?"*

"You shut you so an' so mout', Poodle. You ol' half-blin' bastard. Before I .."

"Keep quiet, Poodle." Clairmonte intervened with a voice like honey. He came over and smiled a smile that was all light and beauty into Congo's bloodshot eyes. "Congo Man, who trouble you now, old Buddy?"

"Don' come skinnin' you teets in my face, Clairmonte. Somebody t'ief my money an' I want it. These people always t'iefing my money, man!" The anger was almost gone. Self pity and righteous hurt now filled his voice. He was becoming truly dangerous.

"They won' leave me alone, Monty. They won'

stop troubling me. They ain goin' stop 'till I do somet'ing to some o' them."

"Hush, Man. You ain' youself. Come, let me take you home."

"Take you so an' so hands offa me, Man. I goin' home when I ready. An' I ain' goin' be ready 'till I see my damn money!"

"Anger transforms men into devils, Clairmonte, and they forget all that they were so painfully taught. They only recognise the urge to strike, to hurt, to 'mash up', to kill..."

"Shut you mout', nuh Poodle."

"....to free themselves it seems from what they have become. To briefly tread the jungle of their birth."

The youngsters at the window laughed. They loved to hear Poodle talking foolishness.

Congo's head was throbbing now. He sat down. He noticed a little white rum left in the bottle. He downed it in one gulp. Then, his hand jerked backwards and the empty pint'n'a-half bottle splat and tinkled on the big rocks outside.

Behind the bar Smoody yawned in disappointment. He had been hoping for an early night. Now this trouble with Congo would surely last until morning. He was not surprised. His expectations were never realised. He had not even planned for this type of existence. His life had not been programmed to take this path. His mother's desire was for him to be a Doctor ... "God's agent in the sacred work of healing and in the wonder of childbirth." She used to say. He, himself had had no special career preference. His life's ambition was simply to be useful, to utilise his talents and energies for the betterment of his fellow humans.

Was he being useful now? Shouldn't he have been allowed to serve in a higher, more meaningful capacity? Had the Sower mistakenly tossed him among thorns and thistles for his essence to wither and decay? Perhaps it had been his own fault. Had he knocked on the right doors? Did he make use of the several good hands he had been dealt? Perhaps the price of success had been too high. Perhaps, the offers he had received and sometimes accepted too often demanded the impossible compromise of his precious integrity - the slow death of his self-respect.

And so he found himself here, in this rum shop. "Smoody, you does buy so much rum from Jonas;" .. they used to joke .. "that he might as well leave the rum shop for you." And their humorous premonition came true. After Smoody had saved his grandson from drowning the old man took him in as an assistant, helped him back on his feet and at his death, entrusted Smoody with all that his life had accomplished.

"SMOODY'S HIDEAWAY", they now called it but Smoody was not hiding.

"There are many roads to hell." Poodle would say. *"The blind and foolish get lost but once. The wise must tread with care."*

Smoody had been lost, or so he thought, on several occasions. He only managed to find himself after he had turned his back on temptation or evil opportunity turned its back on him. Yet, often in his past, the withdrawal pains would hit him and turn his urge for material excess into despair. At these times he could feel the beast within testing with fangs and claws the sagging fences of his self-control. Soon, miraculously, other opportunities would present themselves, opportunities to once more strive unwillingly in the cause of bigotry and greed. Always he refused and suffered some more. They were blind and foolish so he could not join them. They were blind and foolish and yet he could not beat them.

"The many obstacles on the straight and narrow pathway are difficult to surmount and often impossible to circumvent. The weary traveller, when thus confronted must wait, renew his strength and they will disappear."

Smoody transferred his gaze to the pitted concrete floor blackened with ground-in mud. He surveyed the benches and old tables polished with stale sweat and spilled liquor. The pool tabletop, torn and faded. Torn and faded like the souls of those who made their nightly pilgrimage to the musty warmth of this place. Yes, he was indeed a doctor and this was his office. He was a doctor whose prescription never varied whose treatment never failed. They all knew it by heart now and accepted it with relish. The effect of his liquid medicine, taken in unrestricted measure, was swift. Two quick doses would cause lively encounter sessions to organise themselves around the card and domino tables whence, cuss-words and gossip would fly like star lights through the air. All through the evening; all through the room, arguments would erupt about obscure and insignificant topics dissolving themselves into stubborn silence or shrieks of loud laughter. Night after hazy night they would make this pilgrimage retreating only at the approach of a dread and uncertain morning.

"Oh Smoody." Poodle would say. *"Ruler of drunkards, thieves and fools who look to share with you the cup of friendship and love. Know that they but bring with their companionship the scorn and hatred of those respected sinners who dragged you to this foul dock and now would judge you...."*

But he could still win. He was slowly accumulating the money and the courage to go overseas and study medicine. He was still a young man. He could do this and when he came back he would ensure that these, his people were well treated in their years of decay.

CONGO'S STORY

Congo snored causing Smoody to look up .. breaking his reverie. Smoody looked at him. He was sprawled on his back now. Arms stretched out as if he owned the floor. Even in this vulnerable position he commanded his companions' fearful respect. They stepped carefully around, never over, his huge frame. Smoody smiled to himself. Poodle had dared to call this man weak. Poor Poodle. His middle class upbringing would never let him understand. Poor Poodle, if he, with all his intellect, had had to walk through but a portion of the fire that had forged this giant on the floor he would have melted long ago into nothingness.

Congo stirred and pulled himself unsteadily into a chair. His head slowly lowered itself to the top of a table. The crisis was over. The fun could now begin.

"What is Nothing?" Poodle asked.

His brown eyes crinkled in mischievous amusement. The pale, leathery folds of skin on his
cheeks and weathered neck seemed to bulge in an-
ticipation.

"Nobody can't answer?"

Nobody cared to answer. Nobody was in the
mood. Nobody dared answer. Everybody knew
that anything that was said would be enough to
send Poodle off into his own special world of off-
beat argument and weird conclusions. A world
where lesser intellects would drown in a deluge of
beautiful but unintelligible rhetoric.

Besides nobody wanted to talk. It was for them
the dry season. Their heads were always hot; their
parched souls cracked and hard. Nourishment
for them was scarce and ravenous creatures were
about. Their ancestral love of intellectual pur-
suits was now an extinct flower; human affection
only surviving as a sickly plant preserved in alco-
hol.

"Can an ants see a skyscraper?" Poodle persisted.

Clairmonte could take no more. "Poodle, hush
nuh. You can' see nobody ain' taking you on? Nobody in here ain' in the mood for your guessin'
games tonight, man. T'ings brown, man. People
want to study they heads. Fire a li'l drink and keep
your mouth shut."

Poodle was undeterred. "What ails us can not be cured." He said. "Not by our Anger. The time for that is past. And certainly not by our Silence for that is the Cause." He smiled again with drunken goodwill. "You who know nothing know not what Nothing is?"

"Man everybody here know what Nothin' is." Congo intoned from the table top. "Evabody here got it ..... Nothin'. Some o' them ain' got two cents to rub together. Some I know livin' 'pon lumonade and bakes, only buttin' 'bout tryin' to bum two rums an' a cigarette. Looka hush, Poodle, and let a man sleep!"

"An' you ain' much better, Poodle." A woman chimed in. "All you got is that ol' leakin' moses. One o' these mornings I expect to wake up an' hear that you and that gone down."

"Physical, Physical, always the Physical." Poodle waved his hand in a gesture of dismissal. "These physical resources ... fishing boats, cigarettes, rum .. (he poured one) ... are merely the free gifts of our great mother Earth. She, dutifully and lovingly, provides for us in bounteous plenty but we, her ungrateful children have not yet learned to share. We fight and kill each other for what she freely gives. Then we scar and mutilate her in search of coloured stones and the remains of ancient trees. Mankind, I believe, is predisposed to goodness but conditioned to do evil. So we destroy our brothers' bodies and our children's souls. For what? For temporary satisfactions. All is futile, vain and temporary. Let us rest our sports cars and our mansions. Let us rest our yachts and animal skins. Let us rest our divine Money unattended for a short moment on her bosom and our mother will reclaim them all as she will ultimately reclaim us."

There was silence. Poodle was off and running. There was no stopping him now.

"But I was speaking of a far greater Nothing, if it exists. My children, cast your eyes one evening up to the stars. Try to imagine yourself at the very end of the Universe .. at the location of the very last star. What will we find beyond this point? .... Nothing? .. Nothing, you say? But what can this Nothing be? ... What will this Nothing be like?"

His mischievous eyes beamed with satisfaction. He had their attention. They were thinking along with him despite themselves.

"No one can contemplate this, this void. Not even I." He chuckled. "We were not created, it seems, with the mental capacity to grasp such magnificent concepts. My own belief is that this Universe is an infinity, that Life is an infinity. The Journey never ends."

Smoody shuddered. Poodle had to be wrong. The

straight and narrow path had to lead somewhere. No one could journey forever. No one could struggle to overcome the pitfalls and obstacles of existence forever. There had to be something out there. He had to believe that there was a destination somewhere out there, beyond that final star.

He went over and sat next to Congo. He felt the silent welcome. The quiet, warm acceptance. He spoke: "Jonesie you surprise me, man. I didn't know that you cared so much about these people."

"I don't care nothin' 'bout them."

"OK."

Congo raised his head and looked at Smoody's face observing once again the placid expression, the easygoing smile. This new Smoody would always spare himself the trouble of exposing falsehoods; the distress of hurting another person's feelings. He always left it to the liar's conscience to demonstrate in its own nagging way the futility of deceit.

"You all right, Jonesie. You need money?" Smoody asked.

Congo laughed. He always maintained a healthy bank account. "I snug, man. I can't starve."

"Well at least you don't have to worry 'bout the big Nothin' or the little Nothin'."

"Or the medium size Nothin'." They laughed together. Congo poured two drinks and handed one to Smoody.

"But sometimes ...."

"Yes?"

A pause.

"Some mornings", Congo said. "I does feel like if I is a Nothin'. A big wutless Nothin'. Nothin' at all."

The soft brown eyes in the soft dark face beamed warmth at Congo. He perceived the glow. That look had been directed at him since his early schooldays. It had so often helped to repair his heart after the hell of a screaming, bruising night at home. It had been there to comfort him after the torture of a flogging session at school. On many occasions, too, it had been forced to mildly scold him and to still the raging urge he could so quickly feel to destroy all that confronted him.

"Sometimes," he continued. "I does feel like a dog. Like a pet for them perverted people I does mess around. Some o' them does be real strange an' funny, Smoody. Some o' them got some real funny ways."

"Well stop goin' roun' them, nuh Jonesie." It was not a smug statement. It was a friendly suggestion.

"An' do what else man? ... What else can I do? I

nearly famous, Smoody you ain't know. Evabody know me. Evabody know everyt'ng 'bout me. Some t'ings I don' even know 'bout meself. Call any school chil'. Ask them 'bout the Congo Man!" He sucked his teeth. The hurt, angry frown intensified, then faded away ..... He smiled. "Man, Smoody, try and put somet'ing 'pon the table. We ain't had a drink 'pon this house for a real long time."

Different journeys. Different destinations. Smoody felt so helpless. He could see his poor friend speeding down the fast lane on that big, smooth highway. Going where? In his heart he knew that he could always reach out and touch him, their mutual affection was so strong; but it seemed that, in this life, he would never find a way to stop Congo and pull him back.

BUP!

J onesie's father never made sport with women. He dispensed blows at the slightest provocation and at the most inconvenient hours of the night. Last evening, Mrs. Jones had had to be taken to hospital and Jonesie was once more reaching out to Smoody for assistance in relieving himself of the past night's events. Smoody wished he did not have to listen. Accounts of these crude and unfamiliar activities embarrassed him. They caused him to experience a sick and sinking feeling at the pit of his young stomach. But once again, Jonesie's big, sad eyes forced him to pay attention; to try to understand and share the terror and the hurt. The helpless anger.

At last, the story ended. To be forgotten until the next time. A period of pensive silence would pass then, Jonesie would suddenly smile. He would dig into his ink-stained old book-bag and pull something out.. A marble, a top, perhaps a lint covered sugar-cake. Whatever it was they would share it surreptitiously from the secret recesses of their flip-top desks.

"Yes, Parris. What is it?"

"Jones and Smoody have something playin' with, Sir."

They called it Brutus. It lay on the desktop, coiled big and ugly like a giant, leather millipede. Mr. Beckles reached over and picked it up.

"Come up here."

Smoody got up and walked reluctantly to the front of the class.

"I want you too, Jones." There was a hint of impatience in Mr. Beckles' voice.

Jonesie approached them with an air of resignation. He had walked this way many, many times before and he was tired. As he walked his head and shoulders swung involuntarily back and forth as if attempting to shrug off some great burden.

Mr. Beckles brandished the leather strap.

"Why are you boys disturbing my class?"

"We not disturbin' you, Sir." Jonesie whined hopefully. "Don' min' he." He indicated Parris.

"Shut your mouth, boy.... Blackman!"

"Yes, Sir." Smoody said. He tried to speak clearly but his voice was muffled.

"Is there something in your mouth, boy? Come here."

Smoody walked forward. He stopped where his head was now level with Mr. Beckles' 'manager belly'. He could clearly see where it overlapped the waistband of the man's trousers, hiding the belt from view. He could also smell a faint, sickly odour emanating from somewhere in that region.

Mr. Beckles sat on the arm of his chair. He placed the strap back on the desk and used his right hand to pull Smoody closer.

"Let me see." The fat fingers of his left hand squeezed between the boy's upper and lower jaws. Smoody felt the pressure, then the pain. His mouth snapped open. Mr. Beckles' large horn rims peered inside.

"Open up boy.... Oh... I see... Tamarind seeds. You did not have time to dispose of them, eh?" He picked up the strap again.

Smoody quivered. This would be his first flogging. His mother preferred other forms of punishment. Mr. Beckles could see his fear and it seemed to excite him. He placed his hand casually on Smoody's chest.

"Is your heart beating?" He asked intimately.

Smoody did not answer. Mr. Beckles regarded him for a long time. "What a nice, good-looking boy you are, Blackman." He said at last. Mr. Beckles' voice was not high-pitched but it was not deep enough to be pleasing. His enunciation was annoyingly careful. "You belong to a good family. Mrs. Blackman is a lovely lady. You can be an important man when you grow up. Are you going to allow wild boys and riffraff to spoil your future?"

"No Sir."

Mr. Beckles was now sitting sideways in his chair. The youngster's small body was snuggled between his legs. Smoody inhaled cheap perfume as Mr. Beckles bent his ear down to his chest.

"Is your heart beating?" He asked again, this time with an almost shy smile.

"No, Sir."

Everyone laughed but Smoody had spoken the truth. His heart was no longer capable of beating. It had now been transformed into a terrified mouse seeking only to hide its presence from the ravenous beast it sensed without.

Mr. Beckles slowly released his arm. "Go and behave yourself, you hear me. Don't give me cause to call you up here again. No... No do not go back to that seat. Go and sit next to Parris.”

“You heart beatin'?” Parris mocked effeminately as Smoody took the seat beside him.

Mr. Beckles now turned his attention to Jonesie.

“Mr. Jones.” He began grimly. “Why do you come into this classroom late every morning for the sole purpose of disturbing and distracting my good students?”

The verdict was in before the trial and Jonesie already knew what the sentence would be.

“Sorry, Sir.”

“Sorry is not good enough .... Where were you this morning, Jones?”

Hesitation.

“Answer me, boy!”

The loud, angry tone cut through the buzz of the crowded school hall. A hundred or more curious heads turned to see.

“I... I can' tell you, Sir.”

The strap flicked out and tickled the boy’s shoulder. Dust flew from the back of the old khaki shirt.

“Aieeee!” Somebody said and laughed furtively.

“Answer me!” Jonesie said nothing. He no longer seemed to be in the room.

The strap rose and fell. Again and again, with all the force of Mr. Beckles' indignation and punctured self importance. It snaked around Jonesie's shoulders, dug into the sensitive small of his back, stung his buttocks with its burning tip. Other boys would have wet themselves already. Jonesie only stood and waited. To him, cruel punishment was an unwelcome companion whose presence he had learned to endure.

"So you are not crying. You believe you are a vagabond? ... **PARRIS!**"

"Yes, Sir."

"Go and cut me a good tamarind rod."

Fear burned in Smoody's chest. The strap's sting and burn were usually temporary inconveniences but the tamarind rod.. The tamarind rod struck with a dull, heavy hurt. It seemed to aggressively tear the flesh and attempt to crack the bone. It left dark blue weals on the buttocks, the back, the arms. It ...

Parris soon returned, smiling maliciously as he

handed two thick rods to Mr. Beckles.

"Thank you." Mr. Beckles tested the rods. He bent them and watched them languidly recoil. He split the air with them, listening to the whine as he swung them to and fro. After further exam- ination, he chose the thicker of the two, lovingly running his right hand along its knotted length.

"Bend over Jones!"

Jonesie did not move. Mr. Beckles grabbed him by the arm and roughly prostrated him over the desk. He loosened his own tie and began to roll up his sleeve.

"Look out!" Parris whispered.

"So you are a man, eh. Well, you must be satisfied with a man's share."

WHACK! It had to sting. It had to hurt but Jon- esie did not move. No sound issued from his lips. Mr. Beckles might have been beating a pillow. He was not quite sure how to deal with this response. He was already beginning to feel some sympathy, some guilt, but he believed that his credibility and his authority were at stake. He had to press on. He hit the boy's small buttocks again...and again...again and again with all the force he could muster. Splinters flew from the end of the tamar- ind rod.

Mr. Beckles stopped to catch his breath. He wiped

his sweating brow.

"ANSWER ME, BOY! ... ANSWER ME!" There was a hint of desperate pleading in his tone.

"Kill me, Sir." Jonesie said softly. "You have to kill me 'cause you can't make me tell you nothin' an' you ain' goin' make me cry."

It was over. A hundred or more pairs of eyes watched the youngster shrug his way back to his seat. Some watched with admiration, a few with horror. For he was only twelve years old, just twelve years old and already they could see his soul begin to die.

The Question drummed and pounded in Jonesie's brain. It was not new to him. This was not the first time it had thrust itself out of the numbed and frigid confines of his soul. It was a question as original to him as it had been to the millions who had pondered it long before he was born. He, like them was unaware that it had already been screamed and whispered by bankrupt stockbrokers on high balconies; by bereaved mothers and wives, by puzzled professors and unpopular politicians ..... WHY?

When, in the early morning hours he was awakened by his mother's pain-distorted voice and her terror struck the pit of his stomach like a pan of hot water. When forced to view for weeks the bruised and swollen ruins of her face, the 'why' would burn with weak and sullen anger within him. It emblazoned itself upon the hunger and humiliation of his very existence; the mustiness, dirt and vermin, the insults, the brutal floggings.....WHY?

There was no need to hurry. He would be late again for school. But he was in no hurry. Let Mr. Beckles have his fun. Again. But let him wait. WHY oh why did he have to go to school? He wished that his mother would just let him run wild and free until he was old enough to become a 'worthless drunken brute' like his father. She had already convinced him that his head was empty; that his future career would simply be to attend to the needs of racehorses and garden beds. Why then, he wondered, did he have to suffer the boredom and humiliation of two more years of school?

The scent of horse pee and hay now entered his nostrils. He sucked it in. He had been born to it, in a house situated just behind the paddock and from the beginning it had been wafting its unique fragrance into his cradle. As a toddler he would watch in envy as the wild boys who frequented that area gossiped and cussed, striving with their pails and brushes to highlight the beauty of their charges. Often they would come to his window and attempt to coax with candy, soft words and rough tickles some special smile or gurgle from him. The naughtier ones would try to get him to repeat their favourite cuss-words. Once they even tried to frighten him. They brought one of the horses right up to his window; its head was almost as big as his entire body. To their astonishment he reached out his fat little hand to touch the creature. They could not believe their eyes. They hooted and cussed in loud amazement. They were certain that he would have cried.

Now the early morning sun struck him hard between the eyes causing droplets of sweat to pimple his nose and forehead. He wiped them off with the back of his hand grimacing as the wounds and swellings on his back sought urgently to remind him of their existence. The old khaki shirt had become a hot blanket of oppression. He yearned to sit down. He needed to rest.

A ripe mango dropped from the branches above his head, its sudden swish-plop jolting his mind from its depression. The fruit rolled swiftly past him ... a large pink and yellow blob of pleasure exuding as it passed an irresistible perfume. He snatched it quickly from the ground and went over to sit himself down on the grass beneath the generous tree.

He now became aware of the other smelly odours about him. The rushing gutter at his feet told tales of decaying toads, ancient moss and stale bird droppings. The cook shop down the road attempted to retaliate with the sizzling aroma of pork and chicken legs. It filled the air with the scent of frying flesh stuffed with chopped chives, garlic, chilli and black pepper. Soon it would be gone, devoured by the garden 'boys' and the race-horse grooms who congregated there daily to partake of the pork chops and lead pipes, the cut drops and turnovers, the cuss words and the rum.

Jonesie squeezed the mango tentatively; then pounded on its firm body with his fist until it became a soft, juicy 'bubby' in his hand. He bit a small hole in the top of it and sucked contentedly. He was a baby again.

The sweet horse scent from the paddock once more impressed itself upon his mind. He looked across the street. He could see a middle-aged man leading a horse from its stall. Jonesie marvelled at the man's ability to control this huge animal. He wondered what it would be like to be the recipient of so much love and blind trust.

He recalled his very first day at the races. The bugle sound had then blared boldly within his small, new mind as it had arrogantly summoned the parading horseflesh to the gates. It had confidently demanded that all present cease their whiskey guzzling, forsake their Bingo, Tonk and Pokeno and present themselves forthwith to view the impending spectacle. The young men usually required no further urging. They responded immediately to its clear commands, scampering feverishly to perch themselves on flimsy branches and rotting fencing or clambering onto the backs of ancient lorries and donkey carts. Their time for speculation and heated argumentation was past. The bugle had commanded that the next few minutes be spent only in the excited concentration of eyes straining at the distant dust shrouded battle, in finger-snapping screams of hope and encouragement, in pumping backs and thrusting, rocking, gyrating buttocks. This oft repeated ritual would continue until the sweaty bodies and pounding hooves of the horses transported all involved to that moment when the climaxing moans and excuses of the losers would mix with the pleasured screams of those who had been satisfied.

His sister had been forced to take him with her. She paid no attention to his nagging requests. She knew that he would realise in time that he would not be allowed to 'interfere' with the people's bugle. This was his first visit to the races. There would be a lot for him to see, plenty to admire. They had not yet passed the man who reclined himself like an ancient African king in his elaborately decorated chair; his several attendants fanning and feeding him. "Obeah man." Somebody had once whispered in his sister's curious ear but she had not shivered as they had expected. She had seen this man's eyes as she walked past and although they had tried to exude some form of hypnotic power, the lust within them still shone through. She was fifteen. Her body was now beginning 'to turn'. Men whistled and hissed as she walked by. They called her 'darling' and 'honey' and offered her money, clothes and jewellery. She could not at this time understand why any woman would fear a man.

Except perhaps, the 'Bullers'. She feared and despised the 'Bullers'. When she was younger she would laugh with her girlfriends at their wigs and their processed hair; at their exaggerated accents and effeminate mannerisms. It was different now. She was in the final stages of preparation for an unaided plunge into the unknown. She was now tentatively assembling the bits and pieces of the jigsaw that was to be the blueprint for her future existence.

These unusual persons threatened to complicate her simple plans. She had long ago decided that she must take the line of least resistance in life. She would find a man, any man, to struggle her struggle. A man armed with his pick and shovel, hammer and two by fours would be better equipped to battle the daily battle. She might even become lucky and attract the attentions of a bus conductor, or maybe even a seaman. Seamen wore gold rings on every finger and could offer her Yankee money and dresses from Europe. A man had his role, she had decided and she as a woman would have hers... The housework, the meals, the children...

It is true that she envied the freedom men enjoyed to abuse and dominate women and for this reason she found it difficult to understand why these persons would renounce the royal state of manhood to impersonate their mere subjects. Why would a man seek to assume an identity that was in her view merely an extension of his main identity? Why should the all-powerful brain seek to assume the limited functions of a rib? And so she despised these caricatures for the threat they posed to her planned security. She was wise enough, though, to keep her feelings to herself for she had heard that they were very quick to anger and that switchblade knives were often concealed within the clefts of their false bosoms.

Jonesie once more demanded her attention. He had espied a fat, sweating man stirring burst black pudding in a soot-encrusted buck pot. On the shelves above the man, amid the flasks and the nip bottles of Pretty Girl rum and the scattered packs of Trumpeters cigarettes, the coconut punch gleamed at Jonesie like a snowstorm in a bottle.

"I want some o' that." He demanded.

It would be just the thing to keep him quiet for a little while. "How much for the coc'nut punch?" His sister asked the man.

"Three cents a glass, darling.'" The fat man's brain embarked on what he knew was a hopeless fantasy.

She sucked her teeth in mock annoyance but dug into her purse. "Look, I can't spen' all the money I got 'pon you guts. I ain' even went to the shop yet."

"Tek it fo' a penny, then." The fat man said. He wanted her to stay around a little longer.

"It is all right if I buy it fo' he?"

Jonesie probably would have noticed the young man earlier if his attention had not been so completely captured by the jug of coconut punch. He looked at him now and liked him straight away. He was still young enough to be an instinctively infallible judge of human nature and he sensed only love and kindness emanating from this young man. The words had been spoken with respectful shyness and Jonesie believed that it was the youngster's desire to befriend and not to exploit his sister.

She did not answer right away. She pretended to be thinking for a moment but she was slyly examining the young man's dress and features. Eventually, to Jonesie's immense relief, she nodded her head in unenthusiastic acquiescence. She too, was impressed with this stranger but she was well aware of the rules of the game. At this preliminary stage, she could allow nothing in her manner or speech to reveal her true feelings.

"A big one," Jonesie added quickly. He would not be this lucky every day.

The fat man removed a large glass from the shelf and dipped it swiftly into a galvanised bucket. Three lime skins on the surface of the grey water bobbed excitedly as their powerful cleansing and germicidal properties were once more brought into play. He ice-picked a chunk from the slowly melting slab of ice at his feet and, while holding it in his hand, proceeded to split it into smaller pieces with skilful jabs.

"Somet'ing fo' you too?" The young man asked his sister.

"No t'anks." That would be accepting too much, too soon.

"What is the li'l boy name?"

"Tony. He is my li'l brother."

Jonesie forced himself to drink slowly. He wanted to make sure that these two had every opportunity to become well acquainted. The young man had already won his heart and the prospect of more treats like this, an occasional 'berry' and maybe even a regular ride on a bicycle bar was as delicious to him as the creamy beverage in his hand.

"You drinking very slow li'l boy." The fat man said. "You don't like it?"

"How you meanin'?" Jonesie countered.

"Egg...it got in egg. Drink it up it good for you."

Jonesie did not allow this last remark to spoil his enjoyment of the drink. He directed his attention to his sister and the young man. They were chatting easily now and Jonesie observed with pleasure that they had already exchanged names. There was no need for further sacrifice on his part.

He sucked the last of the coconut punch from the glass and handed it back to the man who dipped it once more into the omnipotent grey water and returned it to the shelf.

"You is a joke." His sister said to the young man and laughed happily.

Jonesie surveyed the bustling savannah. His eyes finally came to rest upon an old woman. She sat there, like some black Buddha, on her small wooden bench with her back resting against the side of a neighbouring stall. He noticed that her features were generous and strong, that the bright colours of her bodice blended happily with the black and green around her; that her skirts swirled over and around the tiny bench that supported her huge frame. But it was there beneath the protective overhang of her impressive bosom that his gaze was locked. There in her lap his greedy eyes had discovered a treasure. Row upon alternating row of glistening sugar cakes and comforts ringing the entire perimeter of the wooden tray. It seemed that they were placed there as sentries to guard the toffees, paradise plums and acid drops scattered seductively in the centre.

If he played his cards right, Jonesie thought, he might soon be dipping his sticky little fingers into one of that lady's brown paper bags. He pictured himself popping a morsel of delicious white candy into his mouth. When that vanished like sweet snow under the onslaught of his sucking jaws and probing tongue he would treat himself to the earthy richness of the black.

"COM..FORTS.......COM...FORTS...." The woman sang. She had been taking careful stock of the situation. She was well aware of the possibility of making a good sale. "COM .. FORTS......l'il boy, look the comforts an' sugar cakes."

Jonesie tugged at his sister's long skirts, his face was filled again with distress. "I want......" He started.

But the bugle chose that moment to split the air with its brazen call. Once more the stampede to the rails began. The young man was torn with indecision. Never before had he dared to ignore this summons. He glanced around him. People were rushing as to a fire. Jonesie's sister sucked her teeth in real annoyance. She squeezed herself closer to the stall to avoid the stampeding feet, the swinging arms. In her haste she stepped on an empty soda bottle and started to fall forward. The young man reached out instinctively to steady her and in so doing he experienced the incredible softness of her upper arms, the seductive fragrance of her inexpensive perfume. He decided that he would stay.

Jonesie was becoming impatient. He tugged again at his sister's skirt.

"Yes! What you want?" She was still a little annoyed.

"Look!" Jonesie said and pointed in the direction of the tray.

"What?" She asked. "What it is you want?"

The bugle sounded again this time with almost brutal insistence. The young man was filled with an irresistible urge to obey the summons. He disengaged himself from the counter. He could not afford to miss this race, he told himself. What if something important happened? What if a horse broke a leg or threw a rider? What if some major upset took place? What would be his contribution when the fellows proceeded to debate the occurrence under the streetlight that night?

"Wait here fo' me." He smiled at Jonesie's sister. "I goin' to watch this race an' come back."

He sped off.

"Come!" His sister said and tugged roughly at Jonesie's little hand.

"You not goin' to wait fo' him?" Jonesie asked despairingly.

She sucked her teeth.

"Why not?" Jonesie insisted.

"You t'ink I goin' like a man that t'ink a horse more

important than me? Come along do!"

She dragged him roughly along. He offered some resistance as they neared the lady's tray. He wanted to take one last look.

"Son!....**HOOOOO** ....Li'l boy!...."

His sister stopped for a moment and looked around her.

The lady's broad, country face beamed at them. "Come," she said. He hesitated. She held out a black sugar cake invitingly. "Come fo' this," she said.

"Go 'long," his sister urged. "An' don' forget to say t'anks."

He advanced and took the candy shyly from her hand. "T'ank you." He said.

"Quite." She replied. She was a grandmother. She could not resist the urge to lean over and give him a little hug.

The mango was now a shrivelled sac in his hand. He tore it open and proceeded to rake his teeth along the inside of the skin. When this part of the process was completed he would direct his attention to the hairy, dripping seed. He would lick it and bite at it. He would lick and nibble it. He would lick and suck it until it became white and tasteless in his mouth but it would not be removed, it would not be discarded until he arrived at the entrance to his school.

"BOY! HEY YOU! Why the hell you don' get up an' go to school. You ain' know the bell gone?"

The hand-made book-bag rested on the grass beside him the top of it flipped open and flopped down like a sarcastic smile. The dirty dog-eared pages of the naked exercise books wagging in the breeze like a thousand critical tongues. He opened one of the books and slowly flipped the pages. His eyes viewed dispassionately the several huge crosses, the angry remarks....

"I done school."

"You is fourteen already. Tha' can't be true. You would have to be suffering from the pot."

"I want some work. I ain' want no more school."

It was a slip of the tongue. He had not thought it out. He had not considered the reaction of his mother and father to his seeking employment. He did not expect the man to take him seriously.

"They always want grooms here, man. Go an' talk to the red man in tha' buildin' over yonder."

He was the type to rush in but he never rushed

back out. Not in fear. His actions always supported his words whatever the consequences. He got up and walked resolutely towards the small wooden building not caring that behind him the dog-eared exercise books were slipping one by one into the rushing gutter.

"NO, SEIBERT...NO!"

The fleshy sound of slaps from a heavy hand....Again. The stream of venomous cuss words drowning out feeble protests and embarrassed groans. What was the cause this time? Or did it matter. Perhaps it would be the overused accusation of illicit rendezvous with shadowy lovers. Maybe it had merely become necessary once again for his father to batter down the flimsy barricades set up to protect the source of his satisfaction. Had he been conceived like that? Jonesie wondered. Had he been thrust along with cuffs and curses between his mother's unwilling legs? Had he been, for the past seventeen years a living symbol of her unending humiliation and pain?

He pushed the thought from his mind. He was happy. He was a teenager. He was a man. No one could flog him. No one could abuse him. No one could humiliate him any more. His body lay sprawled in the old easy chair. His head could now rest on the very top of its sloping upper portion; his feet could touch the floor. He remembered when, as a small malnourished boy, his body fitted so well into the centre of that chair that a person entering the room in a hurry would not have noticed him there. Now the huge chair seemed almost too small for his bulging young body. He raised one naked leg and watched with satisfaction as the muscles bunched around his knee. He held it there, admiring the strength and beauty of it, until he was forced by fatigue to let the foot drop to the floor.

He took a sip from the cola bottle in his hand. He had had a hard day at the paddock. A hard, satisfying day. He had come home, taken a quick bucket bath and, clad only in a pair of clean, white briefs had stretched himself out in the big chair. His eyes closed, his mind free to dip and soar in harmony with the slow music oozing from the speaker on the wall above him.

Now again those unpleasantly familiar sounds burst from the bedroom. They seemed to him to be a part of some huge conspiracy; some plot to disrupt his every moment of repose; to keep him perpetually off balance.

"LET ME GO...LET ME GO, MAN!" Jonesie was surprised. This time there seemed to be real defiance in his mother's voice.

The fear he used to feel at times like this had long ago been transformed into anger and disgust. He despised his father. He could no longer respect his mother. He knew that he had been commanded to honour them both but he could feel only revulsion when in their presence. His father he perceived as a weak, loudmouthed bully, too flimsy to withstand the licks of life and too cowardly to grab and break the tamarind rods of his daily existence. A man capable only of projecting his misery on to those innocents who depended on him. His mother he did not understand. She had to be a masochist of some sort. Or a mad woman. No sane being, he reasoned, would so willingly sacrifice her beauty, health and peace of mind for the company of a violent, drunken fool. Maybe she was afraid. Maybe she believed that it was better to accept the difficulties of her present existence than to venture out into a world of unknown horrors. He was young. He was proud and arrogant. He had no time for cowards and fools.

His mother burst into the room now. Her eyes were hot coals of defiance. Her breasts heaved beneath the remnants of her petticoat.

"I mean it man." She shouted. "I had enough o' this now. I tired o' this foolishness, man." Her voice threatened to break but she was able to force it back under control.

"Woman what the hell wrong wit' you tonight?" His father emerged, slamming the bedroom door hard against the wooden partition. He grabbed roughly at her hand.

Jonesie could feel anger and disgust envelop his being. "Wait!" He shouted. "You all can't stop this foolishness now? You all can't see wunna gettin' ol'?"

"Shut you stupid mout'." His father's voice was like thunder. "Nobody ain' talkin' to you. If you don' like what happenin' in this house why you don't leave?"

"I goin' leave but when I ready." Jonesie said.

"When I was you age I would be outside lookin' fo' woman not drawin' up in the house disrespectin' my mother and father. But then again..." his father sucked his teeth derisively, "who woman goin' want a duncy horse head holder like you?"

She would walk along demurely while those beside her giggled at some clever joke or slice of gossip. The neat bodices of their high school uniforms primly restraining new breasts, their starched, pleated skirts disdainfully resisting the determined efforts of the swirling morning breeze. They kept themselves at a safe distance from the contaminating paddock but they could still hear, though they pretended not to hear, the bold hisses, the despairing 'darlings' and complimentary 'lovebirds'. Jonesie would nervously fondle his broomstick at the corner, by the wall. She would pass there, he knew, head high, unaware of his adoring gaze. He pressed himself against the wire to better view her beauty and the broom, forgotten, slipped from his grasp and clattered to the ground. She looked around nervously and came face to face with the devotion in his eyes. For some reason that neither of them could explain, she smiled...

He stood up! "Le' she go, man. Let go my mother!"

His father sucked his teeth and started to pull the woman towards the bedroom.

"Le' she go I say...Le' she....".

The cola bottle flew as of its own volition from his hand. It exploded with an incredible loudness against the partition, inches from his father's head. Fragments of glass and droplets of moisture flew about the room. For a moment there was silence. Everyone, even Jonesie, was surprised. Then his father recovered and rushed at him. His thickly veined hand flew out and thudded, with all the force he could muster, into Jonesie's chest. Pain shot through his wrist as he made contact with his son's work hardened body. He looked up, briefly into eyes that had never before regarded him except with furtive hatred. Now the lust for revenge burned out at him. His weak soul cringed within him as it realised that the little boy had long since gone away. Jonesie did not seem to feel the blow. He raised his hand to strike.

"**NO!**" His mother rushed across to him, her eyes filled with fear and pleading. She gripped his upraised arm with both of her hands trying desperately to pull it down to his side. "NO, TONY...NO, SON, NO!"

"Leh he go!" His father shouted. "Le' he try to hit me if he is a man in here. So help me I will rip out he so an' so guts wit' this." It was his father's favourite knife. Jonesie had seen him use it to sever the heads from hundreds of innocent yard fowls and to emasculate young rams. He used to fear that knife. It had been used as a threat to get him to break the habit of sucking his thumb. He was a child then. He was now a man.

"Touch me!" His father hissed. He pressed the sharp point of the blade against Jonesie's chest. "Touch me, Man."

The sorrow, the remorse, the ifs and buts would all come later. At this moment Jonesie could feel only anger, righteous anger, directed against all those weak, loudmouthed men who sought to bully and bludgeon him into their distasteful likeness. Always. Why did they always have to seek to sacrifice his strength on the altar of their own inadequacies? His swirling brain strained unsuccessfully to register the shouts and whispers of curious and malicious neighbours. He knew that his mother was screaming his name but he could not hear her voice. His body burned again from the sharp sting of the leather strap. His mind churned at the memory of a million insults. His anger frothed to the very limit of his self control and...boiled over.

His hand flew out. He did not try to control the force of the blow. He did not even feel it strike and was barely able to perceive the effect it had on the leering face before him. He struck again and again. The knife shook itself loose from his father's unconscious fingers and clattered noisily across the room. Jonesie's hand darted out. His fingers curled around the fallen weapon. He raised it high in the air.

"NO! TONY...NO!"

◆ ◆ ◆

L ife in prison was to him no different from the life he had known before. Here too were bullies, but braver, tougher bullies who eventually learned to respect his resisting strength and granted him a kind of peace. He remembered little of his stay in that place. He sought to purge the experience from his memory as soon as he was set free. They said that it had been eight years but it could have been eight minutes as far as his numbed mind was concerned. They could have detained him longer. They did not have to let him go. He did not care While there he did as he was told, performing in a robot-like trance whatever menial task, was demanded of him. He did not care. His body did not matter. It was a burden; a slab of dead meat set out in the sun to arouse the appetites of the blue-jacketed vultures and hyenas with whom he was forced to co-exist. He had come to believe that he was only a gatecrasher in this fete they called Life. He had never been invited. His welcome had been cruel and cold.

They finally set him free .. or so they said. In reality they sentenced him further to ramble for weeks about the city; roaming by day through the clean main streets; resting at night in the filthy back alleys. His hair kinky and matted with mud and gutter water; his teeth yellowed and befouled with dustbin rotis and second hand chicken bones. His clothes now rotting with grease and grime barely covered his emaciated frame. As he passed by them, men, women and overripe children would peek in embarrassed excitement at the pendulum swinging provocatively within his torn trousers. But he did not care. His malnourished spirit was close to death and he lacked the means to resuscitate it. He would have welcomed the expiration of his physical existence. Some days he was unwilling to make the effort to scavenge for food. He would lie unmoving on the sidewalk .. waiting to die. Then, one day, as in a dream, he felt hands lifting and gently leading him away. He was too weak to resist. He was only vaguely aware of daily baths being administered, of clean clothes and sheets, of warm soup being patiently poured into his system.

The voice finally found its way into his consciousness. It was deeper than he remembered, richer and more mature, but still kind ... still friendly. Somebody on the outside, a woman, was outlining the dangers of having a madman in the village. The voice that answered her was fearless. It spoke quietly about friendship, about brotherhood, about love...

Love ..... *She passed again by the paddock gate. Her head held high. She neared him and veered a little from her path. Closer now, too close to him, she smiled and in a low breath said: "Good evening." Then hurried in swift embarrassment to rejoin her friends.*

Later, as his mind began to heal, he recognised the face. It was larger but appeared as young as in his elementary school days. The eyes were the only parts of any face that attracted Jonesie's attention. He cared nothing for a cute nose, a sensuous, full mouth when the eyes on that face showed cruelty or weakness. Now slowly, patiently those soft, brown eyes that had comforted him on so many other occasions coaxed and encouraged him again until his befuddled mind and neglected body regained much of their former strength and vigour.

The evening walks also helped. His spirit stirred and soared hopefully within him as he wandered amid the beauty and breezes of the beach. This, he believed, was a new beginning. A chance for him to turn out to be the man he was destined to become.

Whenever he felt especially energetic he would force his feet to fight their way through the sucking embrace of the loose sand so that he could walk between the casuarinas and sea-grapes that grew above the high tide mark. Here he found a world of tangled confusion: of domineering vines, of beautiful, broad-leaved parasites, of huge, black termite colonies glued onto rock faces and rotting tree trunks. This evening he heard a soft giggling and stopped. He looked around, trying to identify the source of the sound. Then he saw them; three schoolboys intently observing some activity in the bushes. He approached them.

"Shhhh!   Hol' down!" They hissed. "Samson got another one."

He bent over and peered further into the bushes. He did not need to be careful. The man and woman were at that stage of their activity when it did not matter to them that they were being observed as long as they were not interrupted. As he watched, he felt a sudden hot hunger rush through his groin. He realised that he was almost thirty years old and had never experienced such sexual intimacy. These pre-teen schoolboys, he knew were probably more experienced in these matters than he. He felt ashamed. He wanted to leave but something kept him riveted to the spot. The woman moaned loudly now. She thrust her hips upwards in greedy demand. Samson chuckled and shifted the weight of his body onto his elbows in an effort to maintain the power and momentum of his assault.

One of the youngsters now decided to crawl silently forward. He slithered to a point where he was almost a part of the activity; where he could smell the smells and hear the sloshing sounds. His cool right hand snaked from the bushes and closed itself gently around the man's turgid scrotum. Samson seemed to lose all control of the lower part of his body. His buttocks spun and whirled like a windmill in a tropical storm. He screamed, then loudly and repeatedly violated the third commandment before sinking heavy and panting on the still moaning woman. The boys burst from the bushes laughing and yelling as they ran down the beach. They would have a lot to tell their little friends tonight.

Samson did not move to pursue them. The woman did not move either. Jonesie could not move. His senses were like nagging children bombarding his brain with questions and demands. The woman finally got up, put on her bikini and ran like a schoolgirl down to the water. Samson sat naked on the rumpled blanket. He groped around for a box of cigarettes, lit one, and puffed with slow satisfaction.

Jonesie started to make his way down from the mound. He crawled slowly and gingerly through

the vines and bushes. When he reached the sand
he stood up and prepared to walk away.

"Tony!"

Jonesie stopped. He did not look behind him.

"Tony. Don't play you ain' answerin' man. I see you
every sence."

Jonesie turned. Samson now in his bath trunks
sat on the top of the mound behind him. The
cigarette dangled brightly from the corner of his
mouth.

"Come, man. I ain' vex. I only want to talk wit' you."

They would laugh and boast in the paddock. This was the best part they would say ... talking about it, especially to poor, suffering virgins like himself. "I like she fo' you," they would say, pointing to some huge woman and would proceed to describe in detail the pleasures they would like her to inflict on his frightened young body. Their vivid stories would mix and mingle at night with his own juvenile fantasies. Try as he might he could not restrict nor control the resulting sweet eruptions and would be forced again and again to hear cautions and complaints from his disapproving mother.

"I don't want to hear anyt'ing."

"Come man. Wait! You frighten fo' me or wha'?"

Jonesie sat down.

"You want one o' these cigarettes Buddy?"

Jonesie shook his head.

"Man, I glad to see you catchin' youself." Samson said . "How t'ings? You workin' yet?"

The thought that he should be providing for himself had not yet occurred to him. He had been in a state of dependency for almost a decade. While in prison he only had to do as he was told and his basic necessities were provided. In the City he had found provisions in alleys, dustbins and at the backdoors of hostels. Nowadays he retrieved rum and beer bottles for Smoody and received food and old clothes in return.

"Not yet."

"I don' have to work." Samson volunteered. "My peoples.." he pointed in the direction of the ocean, "does take good care o' me. This one goin' back to Germany tommor' and I expect a sweet French Canadian to come in Friday." He produced a letter from his clutch bag. "I get this yesterday."

Jonesie could now understand the purpose of the conversation. He had learned, painfully that the prime motivation of any man was that of asserting his superiority over his fellows. To be better in one's own estimation was not enough. That superiority had to be acknowledged by others or demonstrated for all to see. Once this was done the superior one could reach down and bestow some small benefit on his weaker brethren.

The woman, giggling and frolicking in the surf was clear evidence of Samson's machismo. He would now display further evidence of his exalted status. He pulled some money from the clutch bag and thrust it at Jonesie.

"Here. Take this. You goin' need it."

Jonesie made no move to accept the gift.

"Take it, Tony. Do wha' I tell you."

Jonesie did not move.

"Listen, Tony. I know you every sence as a li'l boy in the paddock wit' me. You was always a good little fellow; always willin' to pull you weight and to help out an' I always used to admire you. But face it, man. You life mash up. You can't work an' support youself no more 'cause nobody ain' goin' give you no work. Once a jailbird ... always a jailbird. You know wha' goin' happen to you. You goin either fin' you way back up in prison or you goin' en' up livin' off poor Smoody 'till he get tired o' you an' chase you from he place."

That struck a nerve. That hurt. Would Smoody really desert him? Was that possible?

"Look man. I can understan' you pride. If it was me I might not want to take it neither. Look; I might only be a wut'less, no good he-whore but I know a real man when I see one an' I does admire you. They beat you, Tony, they jail you, an' now they pelt you 'pon the blasted dump heap. I don' know why, but I feel that I jus' got to do somet'ing to help you."

Jonesie's mind whirled. Smoody! He could trust only Smoody. Everyone else despised him...wanted to hurt him.

"Man, look. Take it as a loan then. Pay me back

when you catch you han'." Samson thrust the money into Jonesie's shirt pocket. He expected some reaction but it did not seem that Jonesie had even noticed what he had done.

Samson lit another cigarette. He sucked in deeply then exhaled the smoke with relish. "You know something? You would do good in this business, Tony. The girls would love you. You ain't me .. but you strong, and black an' you got a lovely, big mout'. You would make a real Congo Man."

He laughed at his joke. He felt good. Jonesie had accepted, at least he had not rejected the money and possession of some money always created the urge to have more. Especially easy money. He was certain that after Jonesie had made good use of it he would find that he wanted more.

"The life good, man." He continued. "Look at my hands. No corns, no rough skin...smood an' sof'. I does go in all them big fashion hotels, prance up 'pon the fancy dance floors an' get muh steaks to eat an' lobsters an' all sorts o' big breed drinks. All my Cognac, Irish cream... An' mo' pussy!" He chuckled in glee. "Man I livin' like a king or one o' them Arab Sheiks. Only t'ing is I ain't as stingy as them wit' my oil." He laughed again. Jonesie wanted to laugh too. Memories of the crude conversations and earthy humour of the paddock days stirred in his mind.

Samson could sense the thaw. "Man Tony. Come

an' let me show you the ropes. You got to look out fo' youself buddy. You can't let a bunch o' tinhorns an' poor-great poppets step 'pon you and kick you 'bout all the time."

The woman came out of the water now. She ran happily towards them, arms, legs and unrestrained breasts swinging and flopping in an uncoordinated celebration. Jonesie felt his manhood fighting hard to get at her.

"Sam. I'm ready to leave now." But her eyes were surveying Jonesie with calculating interest. Samson held her lightly by the arm. "Let me introduce you to a friend of mine." He said. Jonesie noticed that he now spoke perfect English with an American accent.

"Hello, I'm Greta." The woman told Jonesie. Her small hand was wet and oh! so soft in his. "What is your name?"

"Tony." He said. Then after a pause. "But some people does call me Congo...Congo Man."

Samson placed his hand with firm, suggestive pressure on Jonesie's shoulder. "I goin' home an' get some sleep. You could walk she back to the hotel fo' me?"

"All right." Jonesie said.

"An' come down by me later an' le' we talk. Okay?"

"Okay." Jonesie said.

The woman lit a cigarette and sat on the sand beside him. "Congo Man." She said. "How interesting. Please tell me more about it."

NORMA'S STORY

C ongo was annoyed but he said nothing. He hated the feel of the woman so close behind him. He hated to have people stand behind him when he played dominoes; especially those self appointed experts who liked to hover like so many half drunk vultures above his puzzled head. They would wait and watch until the end of the game then they would pounce upon him, armed with hindsight, to strip his aggressive veneer and lay bare the bones of his incompetence. He especially disliked Norma. He hated the very sight of her and to have her stand so near to him was distracting, causing him to make even greater mistakes.

Clairmonte stared earnestly at Norma's face but she retained her blank expression. He searched her face for some subtle change that would indicate approval of or disagreement with Congo's game plan. Anything that would offer a clue to the contents of his opponent's hand. But she was too experienced. She knew what he was about and was careful to avoid his gaze. The last thing she wanted was to arouse Congo's anger. She knew that her presence was not appreciated.. that she should leave. Her mind told her that she should go into the kitchen and wash some glasses, fry some fish or something. But she was a woman. She did not always do what was good for her. She was interested in the game but she had a deeper interest in Congo's welfare. She tried to rest her hand lightly on the back of his chair. Immediately there was the sound of wood scraping on the bare concrete floor as the chair hurtled abruptly forward. Congo sucked his teeth.

Clairmonte was at a loss. He pondered deeply for a while.

"Wait, Clairmonte," Somebody said. "You studying law?"

"Man I blocking." Clairmonte said finally. He slammed the six-four down hard on the board in a dramatic action that somehow lacked conviction.

Congo could not believe his luck. For a moment even Norma's irksome presence was forgotten. He smiled and with a flourish revealed his hand. There was no need to count the spots, he was a clear winner.

"Four-love Monty," somebody said. "Congo got you four-love. I would laugh if you let Congo gi' you a six."

Clairmonte knew that his back was getting closer to the wall but he only smiled his sweet, sweet smile.   "Oh, Lord, Congo, You goin' kill muh?" He laughed and carefully unscrewed the cap from the white rum bottle. He poured himself a drink then leaned over and poured a large one for Congo. "Tha' chair like it givin' you luck." He said. "I want a shift."

They exchanged places. Congo was pleased. He was now sitting with his back to the wall. No one could bother him now. Clairmonte was pleased too. He now had Congo sitting right beside the irresistible white rum bottle.

"Clairmonte is a real ol' crow." Somebody whispered to somebody else. "He goin' have Congo playin' foolishness an' mismatching seeds in no time."

Congo looked over to the window where Smoody

sat, waiting. "They comin' yet?"

"No...not yet." Smoody continued to peer intently into the backyard. "I only hope that foolish dog ain' sleepin' again."

"But you would still hear them in the tree." Norma contributed.

"I hear that they fas' an' smart." Smoody said. "Too smart for they own good though. They pick the last o' my fruits."

Norma laughed. Perhaps this time the monkeys had indeed outsmarted themselves. Smoody was an easygoing man. He would have been content with some form of peaceful coexistence with them. He did all he could to accommodate them, mustered all his forbearance. But they seemed, in their senseless, destructive rampages to be impelled by some evil force.

At first, when they took his pomegranates he was surprised and angry. He killed the trees and planted rows of corn. His plan was to reap them early, when the kernels were tender and milky and good for boiling. But the monkeys came before that time. The young cobs had barely poked their soft, silky heads towards the sun when the monkeys attacked. Like the Assyrians of old they tore into the entire patch, "pullin' up an' peltin' 'way" everything they encountered, leaving nothing for Smoody except the loss of his time and labour; the now familiar denial of his expectations.

"They have to eat too." He had told the others lamely when they came to help him survey the damage. But inside he could feel the monster rise and bound, testing its shackles once more for some weak link.

"They want killin'." Congo had said.

The dog had come to slowly rub the length of his body along Smoody's leg. He could sense that his master was upset.

"And where were you at the time, Mr. Dog." Poodle had asked.

"I believe he was outside." Smoody had said.

"Lookin' for what you don't get, Poodle," Clair-monte added.

"He want killin'." Congo said. The dog had snuggled further into Smoody's lap. Congo continued: "Smoody, check wit' me when you want a gun fo' the monkeys, man.... An' fo' he." He pointed menacingly at the dog.

"I di'nt know you had a gun, Congo." Norma said.

Congo ignored her.

And so it had come to pass. Smoody looked now at the rifle resting expectantly on his lap. It had come at last to this. He had made his decision.

His cause was just. Yet his mind could not come to terms with the horrible action it was contemplating. He was a victim of the ultimate devilish ploy, he knew, ... the use of evil means to achieve positive results. They, his invisible enemies, had at last found his weak spot. Tonight he would voluntarily take the first step backwards. Later, they hoped, he would slip and slide further into their grasp.

"The actions of a kind heart, mistook for uncertainty and weakness stand like the restraining pillars of a mighty dam. The slightest flaw may lead to the destruction of this great structure. The tiniest crack may serve to release its hungry waves."

Smoody shuddered. He was afraid. His passion, his intellect, his charisma would make him a magnificent ambassador for evil. It was a constant struggle for him to maintain the placid exterior, the generous and kindly self. Only the love and respect it earned him, sometimes at the most desperate moments, nurtured and sustained his resolve. He did not want to detour from the path he had chosen but he felt that he had to do something even if the action he took should eventually lead him astray.

He would kill them. He would destroy as many of them as he could. The Thought, wild and vengeful, made him sick to the stomach. The Action, when executed, would have a devastating effect on him. Like a virus the evil would spread within his conscience, numbing any sensitivity to his gradual dehumanisation until it ultimately commanded his soul.

He cast his eye to the withering branches lying on the ground. His mother had planted that guava tree. Her old hands had trembled as she placed the small, leafy stick in the ground and carefully compacted the dirt around the hair-like roots. He had seen her struggle beside it against the indifference of the poor soil, against the onslaught of slugs, fungi and pests of all descriptions. For months she had attended the silent creature until finally it had responded to the irresistible power of her love. It started to grow. To spread itself and fling its smooth, hard limbs to almost every corner of his backyard.

In those dark years that were to follow, the searing heat of his existence, the pressing load of his disappointments would chase him to the shade of its whispering leaves. He would rest beneath the tree and remember .. his heart sad with loss and yearning yet filled with wonder and gratitude. He would cradle there in its shelter and support, his mind sucking strength from her ever-living spirit and her never-dying love.

There was the crashing sound of branches bending and recoiling a little way off. The same sound that his beloved mother's guava tree had made as the vandalising monsters ripped and tore at it. The same sound that had firmly implanted this murderous desire in his gentle heart.

"Shhh!" He said. "Out the lights somebody."

They turned out the lights. Moonlight filtered in from the yard. Everybody crowded around the window to see. Soon they heard a series of low warning sounds.

"Look he there!" Somebody whispered.

"He big!"

The creature swung lightly onto the sugar apple tree. It looked around warily, then, satisfied that the coast was clear, it emitted a series of low grunts. Now other monkeys appeared, the young ones darting playfully through the bushes, the muscular old fellows striding with a graceful arrogance over the branches. The first monkey to appear sat casually on a branch. His hairy arm darted out.

"You mean he had to bre'k off the whole bough to pick one sugar apple?" Smoody muttered.

The creature did not seem to be satisfied with that particular fruit. He dropped it to the ground and swiftly picked another.

"Wait, you goin' le' he pick all o' them," Congo

hissed. "Shoot the damn t'ing, Smoody."

The weapon was cocked and ready. The muzzle was aimed directly at the creature's chest. The trigger snuggled suggestively beneath his finger. Smoody's anger swelled as he watched them swinging gleefully about the tree dropping half-ripe and half-eaten fruit onto the ground. Another part of him thrilled reluctantly to the way they sat together, lovingly sharing their simple treat like children at school. He wanted badly to be rid of them but try as he might, he could not summon the Thought that would blot them out of existence.

"Smoody wha' happen?" Clairmonte asked.

Congo snatched the gun. "Move, man!" He said. "You like you frighten."

He sat down and took careful aim. The big monkey now skipped lightly to a higher branch. Congo waited for it to settle down.

It was then that Norma felt the hand beneath her skirt. Maybe it had just commenced its explorations or maybe she had been so preoccupied with the unfolding drama that she had not noticed it before. It was a man's big hand. It passed with a shy, circular motion over and around her buttocks. She could feel the heat of its excitement through her panties. Her skirt rose and fell as the arm pushed surreptitiously up and down. She stiffened. The hand froze, awaiting her further response. Her shocked silence seemed to signal acceptance. An emboldened finger squeezed between her legs, forcing aside the protesting elastic of her undergarment and flicked tentatively at where it guessed her clitoris might be.

The old fear, the old hurt, the old nausea enveloped her. For a moment she was certain that it was him. Again. Then she came to herself but forgot where she was. **"WAIT!"** She shouted loudly. "Who it is feelin' me up? Wunna t'ink I is a blasted fowl?"

The monkey leader issued a dub song of urgent, guttural commands. His family jumped and scampered from the tree. Congo cursed and fired twice. Everybody jumped as the deafening report of the rifle sounded above the crash of leaves and branches and the loud screeches of the monkeys as they hastened in wild panic from the yard. The dog woke up now and proceeded to add a variety of yaps and growls to the ensuing racket.

Congo turned on Norma. "You foolish bitch!....You couldn't keep you blasted mouth quiet?!" He raised his hand as if to strike.

"Take it easy, Jonesie," Smoody said. "Take it easy."

Congo walked away.

"Smoody, I sorry." There were tears in Norma's big eyes. "But.... you understand...Right, Smoody?"

"Yes, I understand..."

Then there was the scream - so terrifyingly unexpected, so eloquently clear. There in the full moon, she bawled her grief and loss, frantically proclaiming the recent brutality of these humans to any listening power that might avenge her. With prodding claws she willed life into the still and bleeding body of her infant but to no avail. Tears gushed in white profusion from her eyes. From somewhere in the bushes she heard a warning call but she could find no room inside of her for fear. Once again she issued her deafening and heart-rending screams turning to face her tormentors with defiant anger in her eyes. Then, finally, she scooped the small, lifeless body to her breast and disappeared, still howling, into the trees.

Smoody turned to look for Norma but she had already fled the room pursued he knew, by her constant companions ... the ghosts and demons of a million past nightmares. Tonight, again, they would ride and taunt her. They would force her to relive and relive the sinful tragedy of her past, trying their evil best to destroy the remnants of her sanity. Smoody prayed that she would not let them win. He hoped, he believed, that some morning soon it would all begin to change.

Norma laughed loudly but she laughed alone. It seemed that this anecdote amused only her. Her young friends preferred raunchier jokes. They liked to be titillated and tantalised by more explicit tales of outside women and foolish men than this. Mingy fancied himself as a storyteller and he knew that he had a tough and demanding audience. He would only slip in a loser when he had trouble remembering his better material. Indeed the youngsters, assembled on the front step, knew many of the jokes better than he did but they liked the way he told them. And so, whenever they realised that he was starting to dry up they would assist by requesting "the one about the cou-cou stick" or "the one about the two micies" and Mingy would be off and running again.

Dusk was that time of day when juvenile pastimes gave way to their continuing lessons in the strange and amusing world of adult sexual practices. They would congregate every evening on the front steps of an abandoned house and hope that Mingy would decide to pay them a visit. As soon as his huge, khaki-clad frame was seen approaching them all the hopscotch, skipping and marble cricket would cease. Those unfortunate hiding hoop participants who had been too clever in the choice of their hiding place ran the risk of being lost forever or could feel free to indulge in the other variation of that popular game.

They laughed. They enjoyed themselves. Of course they knew better than to believe that the ridiculous situations Mingy related were true. They had already been exposed to promiscuity, to infidelity and the oft resulting brutality. These evening anecdotes served to soften the impact of real life situations and the shared laughter helped to purge the residue from their young souls.

Mingy was a handyman. He performed odd jobs for everyone in the village ... weeding, attaching handles to old tin cans thereby creating those multi-purpose utensils called 'tots'; helping to dismantle and reconstruct houses. Everybody liked him and he liked everybody. He was always charming and amiable. When he had in his 'waters' he would stagger up to regale any small group of people with his cleverly coined big words and inoffensive picong. It did not take long for him to attract attention. Heads would pop from side windows and galvanised gates would creak open as the impromptu sideshow got into high gear. He was a child at heart it seemed. He amused his audience and they brought meaning to his lonely existence.

This evening, though, Norma was not fully

amused. Her recent laughter only momentarily dissipated the uneasy feeling she had experienced a few moments earlier. Her puzzled mind recalled the violated sensation that had surged through her as Mingy ran his raspy hand down her leg. She had tried to make excuses for him. He was not drunk, she knew, but he had been drinking. Perhaps he had only been trying to steady himself. She had almost convinced herself of this when she once more felt the hand's hot weight on her naked skin. Again the puzzled, uneasy feeling rushed back to bother her.

It preyed for weeks upon her mind. She was not ready for this. Not yet. Not at thirteen. Her source of pleasure was in skipping rope and pitching marbles. She still enjoyed playing with her dolls... shopping for them with 'cut plate' money and feeding them mud cou-cou. She was not ready for womanhood. She was still being prepared. The fact that two puny hog plums had somehow attached themselves to her chest did not suddenly transform her mental state to that of a mature woman.

The situation did not frighten her. It puzzled her. She did not need Mingy's vulgar anecdotes to introduce her to the dynamics of sexual relationships. She had only to open her little eyes to observe men pissing on walls and clawing suggestively at their privates during conversation. She had only to allow her ears to absorb the sexually instructive cuss-words spewed in jest and anger into the village air. Sex was no mystery to her. Her little friends would tell their tales of 'rudeness' performed or witnessed and she had often heard from adult lips how Mr. Blades had come home one day too drunk or too excited to remember to shut the front door providing a free 'floor show' for those bold enough to watch.

No. She had not been sheltered. She had been forced by economic circumstances to mother her small brother for the last four years. She had been aware of his existence even as the first grunts and moans of conception filtered through the thin bedroom partition in their house. She had weathered the discontent of gestation. She had been the one who had run to arouse and summon the midwife and had afterwards shared in the suffering and joyful accomplishment of his birth. Now she cared for him. She nursed his every minor ailment. She loved him. One day, she too would experience in her own right, this alternating cycle of pain and joy. She was not afraid for she sensed that it was her blessed privilege. But she was not ready. Not yet.

The men thought differently. They began to notice that the little snotty-nosed creature they once chased in mock anger from the vicinity of their card games was being transformed into a different being designed to bring them pleasure. The appearance of these two lumps signalled the discovery of a new frontier, a virgin country. Who would be first to sail to its shores? Which lucky man would hammer down his victorious flagpole and stake his claim to its exclusive exploitation?

Every man in the village fancied his chances and planned his strategy to suit. Some of them observed her passage with shrewd, calculating glances, devising ways and means of grasping the prize while avoiding the concomitant pitfalls. They were willing to plant the seed but did not want to labour for years in the harvest. Others, less cautious, coaxed and cajoled her openly with loud insincere compliments and the jiggling of coins. This sudden, new attention was often upsetting to Norma. Her harassed mind sometimes screamed to her body to cease its bold march into womanhood and to retreat into the complacent existence of a child.

Mingy too, was drawn to her; not so much by the competitive instincts of the other men but by his own unfulfilled natural urges. He was in his early forties. He had no woman friend and his opportunities for sexual fulfilment were few. His days were pleasantly spent in the sun, and the rain, poking, pulling and prodding fruit trees and flowering plants into shape. His evenings were dedicated to the amusement of his neighbours and his rum-drinking cronies. His nights, his sober nights, were often cold, bleak periods of yearning and despair.

He could get a woman of course. Every piece of cloth has its owner. But he did not care for the shop-soiled material that would often try to thrust itself upon him. He despised the promiscuous, foul-mouthed creatures who frequented the rum shops and dance halls. He had a mother, and sisters. He had a profound respect for women. He found it difficult to understand how these persons could so debase themselves, their relatives and their children.

The women he desired, the silk and satin of the village, would never drape themselves over his broad shoulders and between his muscular legs. To them he was only a loveable buffoon, a convenience to be given a few cents and a plate of food after he had done their gardening or swept their backyards. He had his place and they had theirs. To stoop to touch him would be to risk eternal scorn. But young, inexperienced Norma might not be so discriminating. Mingy was shrewd enough to realise that he had an advantage over the other men; he could exploit his access to the girl. He was not unaware of the moral and legal restrictions her age and immaturity presented but he was a man driven by seemingly uncontrollable desires. Any moral qualms were dissipated by the succulent visions of her emerging sensuality. They interrupted his slumber night after night. He answered only to the need, the gnawing hunger inside him. Her silence after the act was his only concern and he believed that this could be purchased. He was a thrifty fellow. It was rumoured that he had old tots of money buried all over his backyard. He was willing and able to pay. He was willing and ready to do anything that would allow him to pop those two half-ripe hog plums into his starving mouth before the other encircling blackbirds could swoop upon them.

He therefore prepared even spicier anecdotes featuring the exploits of lovable and generous older men as they outfoxed their clumsy young counterparts. He made a show of buying sweets and soft drinks for the members of his young audience. He would bring them crocus bags full of mangoes and guavas; bunches of ackees and huge hands of bananas that he would obtain from the gardens he tended. He always ensured that Norma received the choicest and the best and rejoiced to see her laughing at the jokes, sucking contentedly on the sweets and chocolates and munching on the fruit. She would recoil, he noticed, and change her place every time he attempted on whatever pretext to touch her body. But he was undeterred. She would change her attitude in time.

A teenager's life can often be a time of great unhappiness. The tension created by the often blatant sexual advances made upon her now caused Norma to be even more sensitive to the other negative forces in her life. Her father's attitude, for instance, often annoyed her and as she grew older she began to be bold enough to let her displeasure show. She could not understand why he allowed himself to walk past the several rum shops lining the route only to discover the need for rum or cigarettes on his arrival home. She was no longer eager to rush to the shop on these errands in the hope that she would be allowed to purchase some treat with the change for she now had to look forward with distaste to the unwelcome attentions of the men who loitered there.

Now he wanted cigarettes again. Norma did not want to leave the house that evening but she was not willing as she had often heard it said to 'take licks' rather than run the errand. She slammed the back door loudly though, as she departed and listened with resentful satisfaction to the angry protests of those inside.

She sucked her teeth as she approached the alley. She hated having to pass through that alley. These days she always felt so harassed and threatened that the thought of passing through the alley at dusk filled her soul with fear.
The alley provided a short cut to the nearest shop. It was a white, rocky path between a barbed wire fence and a rusty galvanised iron paling. It was the rainy season now and clumps of white head bush and nettles sprouted along its untrammelled edges. Above them, wild tamarind and stinking toe trees battled for space while slender coconut

palms swayed complacently on high, occasionally bombarding anything below with shrivelled and unwanted nuts.

Norma now peered fearfully into its darkness.. She could imagine 'heart men' in the shadows expectantly fondling their knives. The rustle of mongooses and mice in the dead leaves now became the malicious manoeuvrings of duppies and hags. Caught between the proverbial rock and deep blue sea, she knew that she had to go on but she desperately yearned to turn back. She felt the urge to cry.

Her eyes had all this time been adjusting themselves to the dim light and were shocked to view the indistinct profile of a man standing motionless at the other end of the alleyway. The man was using his bent left arm to protect his head from the rough trunk of a palm tree. His right arm hang downwards, limply holding on to a long, dark object. **"HEART MAN!"** Norma thought. "Well he ain' cutting out my heart wit' that knife tonight."

 She turned to run away but curiosity forced her to stay and watch a little longer. The man was not close enough to cause her any harm. There was no way he could reach her before she scurried back inside the house. She was too fast... and too frightened. The man now pushed himself laboriously from the tree. He proceeded to shake the 'knife' violently for some time. Finally he replaced it inside his trousers and began to walk, somewhat unsteadily, in her direction.

As he got closer she began to recognise the walk. Soon she was able to identify the features. It was Mingy. She had often seen him in the rum shop drinking and joking with his friends. His presence in the alleyway encouraged her to press on. At least she would be safe on the outward journey. On the return trip she would just have to make a quick dash for home and hope for the best. Mingy was walking so slowly and unsteadily that Norma had almost reached the top of the alleyway before they met. He was drunk she could tell. He exuded a strong smell of rum mixed with fresh male sweat. He recognised her now. His face registering both surprise and pleasure.

"Norms?" His voice caressed the name. "What you doin' outside so late?"

"I goin' to the shop fo' somet'ing." She said, and started to walk past him.

"What it is you goin' for? You want me to buy it fo' you?" His intoxicated state caused his words to have an almost silly ring to them. He rocked and swayed as he attempted to retrace his steps.

"Uh, Uh. I got enough money." She again started to move away.

He reached out and held on to her arm. "Norms, please! You don' treat me right, you know."

What did he mean? She thought. She was not qualified to satisfy his requirements. She was only a child.

"Tell me what you want. Anyt'ing at all you want I will gi' you," he pleaded. "Tell me, nuh?"

She had never before been exposed to such vulnerability. She had heard about it, this awesome female power that could "turn men bewitch" and force them to walk the streets every day without a destination. But she was too young for any of this. She could feel only pity for this poor man. He possessed a body strong enough to destroy her with a single blow, yet her mysterious female charms were forcing him to grovel at her feet.

She had to leave. She started to pull away but she had tarried too long. He had misinterpreted her hesitation. She felt herself being pulled towards the hardness of his body. Her own body did not possess a fraction of the strength required to render effective resistance. "Let me go!" she started, but it was too late. She became acutely aware of the rum and sweat filling her nostrils as his hungry mouth descended to cover hers.

It was awful. His saliva was a sewer of stale rum and tobacco. She could feel his large tongue trying to force its way between her clenched teeth. She tried to scream and it managed to slip through to thump at and tickle the roof of her now open mouth. Mingy grunted softly then so tightened his grip on her that she now found it difficult to breathe. His hands were now massaging the soft globes that were her buttocks. For a brief moment she marvelled at their masculine roughness. Then she panicked. She rocked and struggled despairingly against him. Her strenuous movements caused him to take an unsteady step backward. His foot found a loose stone, his ankle turned over causing his upper body to fall heavily against the galvanised iron paling.

"*Y gaz!* Who out dey?"

Norma struggled some more. The paling crinkled musically in protest.

"I say who dey?" The voice threatened to alert the entire neighbourhood.

Mingy pressed his hand firmly over Norma's mouth.

"It is only me Miss Pear. Mingy. I now gettin' in."

"Mingy? Mon Dieu! If you don' stop drinkin' you soon will have to buy me a new palin'." Mrs. Pierre laughed pleasantly.

"Sorry, Miss Pear. I sorry."

"Try an' get home safe you hear?"

"All right, Miss Pear. Good night."

"Good night, Mingy."

Mingy had by now sobered somewhat. He looked down to see the young girl's puzzled tears. His partly satisfied passion gave way to remorse and self disgust. He realised that she was but a child. A child hurt and crying, punished for his crimes, suffering his suffering. His selfish desire transformed itself into a tender, protective love.

"I sorry."

She did not stop crying.

"The rum," he continued. "I was a li'l tight, Norms I di'nt know what I was doin'."

She scalded him now with eyes that spoke of terror and distrust.

Suddenly, the fear of discovery gripped him.

"Don' tell nobody 'bout this. Please! Promise me you won't tell nobody. I won' do it again. I swear."

He, too, now seemed on the verge of tears.

She began to straighten her clothes. He continued to beg in a low voice for her silence and forgiveness. She ignored him and walked on toward the shop. She had already decided to keep this incident to herself. She could do without the scoldings of her parents and the gossip of her neighbours and friends. But she would also keep this decision secret from the pleading Mingy. She would let him suffer. She was beginning to enjoy this woman's power.

After this Mingy could not be found to entertain. His loud guffaws and cheerful greetings no longer rang through the village. He sought employment now on the spacious lawns and huge gardens of the rich inhabitants of the Terrace and could no longer find time to perform odd jobs for his neighbours. He became a fleeting shadow, darting to and from his home after dark and before the sun could rise.

"I can't fin' Mingy." Norma heard her perplexed mother complain to Mrs. Pierre.

"I ain' see him fo' some time meself." Mrs. Pierre set her tray down with great effort. She proceeded to adjust the circular padding on her head.

"He like gol'." Norma's mother continued. "An' I want him to weed roun' the place for Christmas."

"Yo' 'usban' can't do it?"

"Seibert?!" Norma's mother sucked her teeth. "I really wonder wha' happen to Mingy." She started again. There was genuine concern in her voice.

"Don' worry. I sure he all right." Mrs. Pierre said. She had to make her rounds. "How much mango you say you want?"

Time passed and the grass kept growing. Norma's mother decided she would have to try to clear it herself. She arose earlier than usual one morning and had just begun to peck unenthusiastically at the lush growth when a distant, furtive figure attracted her attention.

"Mingy!...Hooooo! Mingy!"

Her voice, happy and relieved shrilled loudly in the early stillness.

The figure turned and tried to slip between two houses.

"Mingy!....Mingy!...Wait. I want to talk to you."

He could avoid her no longer. He turned like a condemned man to hear his fate. She could see fear and anguish in his eyes.

To his surprise she smiled at him. "Mingy. Wha' happen to you, man?"

"I all right, Miss B." He forced himself to say.

"But wha' happen to you though? You like you did los'. You went to Los Angeles?"

She expected at least a smile in response to this borrowed witticism but there was no animated reply, just an uncertain shake of the head.

Norma came to the window now. Mingy could not see her through the blinds but she could observe him and the effects of her silent torture.

"Mingy, wha' happen to you, man. You sick?" Her mother persisted.

"No. Miss B. I ... okay."

"Well it is very strange that you don' come to see we no more. Look. I want you to weed roun' the place for me. When you comin'?"

Early next morning a surprised Norma was awakened by the scraping and chopping sounds of his hoe and cutlass. She lay in bed and listened for a moment. She knew that she should not have been surprised. Only her father, it seemed, could resist her mother's charm and inner beauty. Everyone else, workmen, hawkers, dressmakers were forced to succumb to the bargaining power of her smile and to melt beneath the warmth of her personality. This however was only part of the reason for Mingy's hasty response to her mother's request. The sensations of that roughly stolen moment in the alleyway had not receded in his memory as they had done in Norma's. He took them to bed with him every night. They had by this time germinated and developed into sweet fantasies that would sweep him to the very pin-nacles of pleasure. But there was always the fall. For just as his clawing hands and pumping feet succeeded in transporting his body to the edge of erotic fulfilment, his mind would slip and dash him abruptly into the abyss of shame.

Now as he hacked and pulled at the nut grass and the hug-me-close he hoped that Norma would somehow appear. He wanted to observe her. To see if his actions had had any long term ill effects on her. He needed some sign of recognition from her, any small crumb that would begin to set his mind at ease.

He made good progress in the cool early morning. The soil was damp from recent rains and the bushes offered little resistance to the strength of his experienced hands. Now, the sun was climbing in the sky and warming the air around him. He could feel it begin to suck the energy from his body. His enthusiasm waned.

"Mingy don' kill yo'self in the hot sun now you know."

"Soon finish Miss B."

It was a small area. He would only require about fifteen more minutes to complete the job.

"Norma. Take this jug o' lumonade out there an' gi' Mingy some for me."

"Ma. I doin' somet'ing."

A brief session of scolding and bleating protest ensued.

"It is all right Miss B." He hastened to make peace. "I all right. Soon finish."

"She have to do as I say. She ain' no woman yet. Not in here."

A sulking Norma soon appeared with the pitcher of lemonade and some sweet biscuits on a tray. It was as he had feared. Her face and carriage revealed that confused and rebellious mental state so common in adolescence. Once again he was the cause of her suffering. Her fierce, young anger was once more directed at him.

"Here." She said, and dropped the tray on the front steps. He was certain that she fed her dog more graciously.

She was anxious to leave right away but she knew that her mother and good manners would demand that she should wait until he was finished. She made a show, though, of turning her back on him until the ordeal was over. Mingy did not want to prolong her discomfort. His uneasiness at the thought of a confrontation with her had vanished as soon as she had appeared. He now felt happy for some reason. His heart felt a new lightness, not the forced jollity he had so often projected in the past, but a real and sincere happiness. He knew that she wanted to get away, and he decided to try not to detain her. He quickly filled the old plastic tumbler she had brought and downed the contents. He did not realise that he had been so thirsty. He poured another glassful and drank it more slowly. She remained with her back to him and this enabled his mind to unashamedly register and record her changing beauty for future moments of private contemplation.

He picked up a few of the biscuits and stuffed them into his shirt pocket. Then he removed the tray from the step and presented it to her with a gentle flourish.

“Come,” he said softly.

She turned slowly and defiantly to take the tray from his hand, forcing herself not to show the shock she felt as she briefly surveyed his face. He seemed to have aged. The friendly charm seemed to have been washed away. The face appeared thinner and deep wrinkles were now gouged into his forehead. She tried to transfer her gaze but his eyes held her spellbound for a moment with their intimate revelations. From their dark depths some benign being beamed invitingly at her. She felt her spirit stir in response. She had not been accorded such humble recognition, such unabashed adoration since before she had forsaken her mother's arms to crawl upon the floor.

“T'ank you.” His voice was a soft whisper. She did not reply immediately. She waited until she reached the corner of the house. Then she turned.

“It is all right.” She said and disappeared from view.

“Mingy.” Norma's mother called. “The lumonade

sweet enough?"

"An' you ain' make it Miss B? Anything you make would have to be sweet."

◆ ◆ ◆

Time passed and with its passing healed and washed away the scales and scars caused by the memory of that encounter in the alley. The thirteen year old's terrifying nocturnal adventure became the fifteen year old's joke. In moments of idle reflection Norma would giggle at this and related memories, like her fear, in the days after that incident to leave her home in the evening. Her father's violent displeasure did not at that time, serve to weaken her resolve. She would cry pitifully, whether he flogged her or not. He finally managed to remember to procure adequate supplies of rum and cigarettes before he reached home.

She also remembered her reaction the time her little brother had playfully sneaked up behind her and slapped her hard on the buttocks.

"Gotcha." He had shrieked in glee.

Her terror had not recognised his little voice, his smiling face, until it was too late. It had spun her around and had caused her right hand to shoot out with surprising speed and slam itself against his cute little head. His shrieks of pain then caused sanity to rush back into her whirling brain but the damage had been done. Her kisses, her coos, her promises of sugar cakes and sugar plums, none of her enticements could restore the fraction of love and trust so violently dissipated. For weeks afterwards, she could not raise her voice in his presence without exciting a cringing reaction. Time, however, once more worked its magic and as the stinging memories retreated to the rear recesses of his consciousness he once again felt free to fill her days with joy or frustration as the spirit moved him.

At fifteen, she had now become appreciative of her ripening beauty and thrilled to the attention it brought her. She developed an intense interest in her appearance. She nagged and pleaded until she was allowed to straighten her hair. She would have liked to be taken to a professional hairdresser but had to be content with her mother's old coal pot and ironing comb. She ensured that no wrinkles were allowed to spoil the appearance of her school uniforms. She ironed them every day and when sitting in class she would carefully arrange the skirts around the bench in order that the pleats would remain intact. The deportment badge she received for her efforts she pinned in a position where it effectively highlighted the slope of her still emerging breasts.

The male attention she enjoyed most of all. While she relished with haughty detachment the many juvenile efforts to win her favour, she would offer nothing more than a serene and friendly smile. She was an intelligent girl. She understood that a sign of commitment given to any one competitor would only serve to enhance his situation and diminish her own power. She was no fool. She would parade her regal self past the whistles, the sweet eyes and the admonitions. But she would not play her trump card until the game was coming to an end.

There was one dark lining to this silver cloud. Lolita Jordan pretended to her throne. Lolita Jordan was a girl of undeniable beauty but of doubtful chastity and intelligence. There was the mutual dislike of juvenile competition. The passing sniggers, the catty remarks. There were the fights … brief, noisy affairs guaranteed to delight the vociferous male audience with tantalising glimpses of soft legs and big, blue, puffed-leg panties. After the pulling, the shrieking and the scratching had been quelled by the intervention of some authority figure, the resentments would be left to simmer until the next eruption.

Then Lolita Jordan got earrings. Gold earrings. They were long gleaming, raindrops that would shoot sparks of blazing light into every envious eye. Golden whips for Lolita Jordan to fondle and crack, suppressing and humiliating the naked ears of those around her.

"Norma, you see Lolita earrings yet?" Shirley asked her.

"Yes. Who ain' see them ain' livin'."

"You right. The way she does get on sometimes does make me feel like pullin' them off you ain' know."

"Fo' what?" Norma sucked her teeth in mock indifference. She was aware that Shirley was a back-biter. She had to choose her words very carefully because she knew that every one of them would to repeated to Lolita and her crowd. But she was indeed jealous. She felt in danger of losing her exalted position. She decided to give Shirley a juicy bone to take back with her.

"I would 'ave had some better ones than them every sence but I frighten to get my ears pierce."

"Girl piercin' you ears ain' nothin'. Come down by me after school an' le' me do it fo' you."

She had seen it done to others. She had seen grown women bite their lips in trying not to cry. She had heard little girls scream and utter profanities they were not supposed to know. The prospect of the stinging pain as the hot needle violated her ear-lobes did not appeal to Norma but she found the thought of an earringless life spent in the shadow of Lolita Jordan's glory to be even less appetising. She decided that she would have it done.

Shirley was an ugly and insecure girl, but she was skilful. It was said that she could find a way to bone spiders if she put her mind to it. She had performed this operation many times before. First she ensured that each earlobe was properly benumbed with chunks of hard ice. She carefully sterilised the needle with the flame from a safety match. Then, with the skill of a surgeon, she slowly inserted it into each lobe. Norma was relieved. There was no blood and very little pain. Shirley next threaded a thorn from the flat hand cactus into each hole to keep them open.

"You goin' have to make sure it keep clean." She advised.

"How long before I can put in the earrings?" Norma asked casually.

"'Bout two weeks if it don' turn out."

Norma secretly hoped that the two weeks would be enough time for God to work some miracle on her behalf. She had no gold earrings to place in the newly pierced ears and was not about to receive any. She could only hope that this little blarney would save her some face until the novelty of Lolita Jordan's earrings wore off.

But she overplayed her hand .... ducking from everything that passed within a metre of her head; describing in detail the dimensions and intricate ornamentation of the imaginary jewels she was soon to wear. She even went so far as to 'lowrate' her rival's earrings and to predict their imminent discoloration. Lolita Jordan had no ready response to these tactics. She doubted whether Norma possessed what she was professing but she could not risk voicing her suspicions. She decided to play a waiting game. She would give Norma all the rope she needed. This new game was not to end in stalemate but in total devastation.

As time passed, Lolita became more and more convinced of the accuracy of her suspicions. She however, still maintained her cautious attitude and would limit herself to dropping remarks as Norma walked by.

"Them is the new style, you ain' hear? Plimpler earrings is the in thing, girl." Or: "Wait! She loss them fancy new earrings she get a'ready. I di'nt even get to see them."

Norma would burn with shame as she tried to ignore the howls of derision and shrieks of malicious glee. Only Shirley would chat with her, grubbing in her cloying way for some new morsel of gossip. Today she was pretending to examine Norma's ears.

"Norma them heal now. You can put in the earrings now."

"You sure?" Norma hedged. "I frighten them t'ings rotten off my ear or somet'ing."

"Them ain' gol'?" Shirley asked hopefully. "I t'ought you say them is gol'."

"Yes! Eighteen carat."

"Well gol' don't harm you skin. Look. Try an' put in the t'ings, do. You goin' let Lolita Jordan make you a mock stick all the time?"

Norma's mind raced. The most important thing in the world now was the acquisition of a pair of eighteen carat gold earrings. If she did not produce them soon her whole life, it seemed, would be over. It was hopeless. She would just have to pull these two "plimplers" from her ears and try to endure the humiliation that would follow. She could feel tears start to moisten her eyes.

"So tell me." Shirley was saying. "When you goin' put them in?" Shirley's words were chosen to convey the impression that she believed Norma's story about possible damage to her ears but her eyes, her posture told a different story. She wanted a climax, a deadline date after which she could snigger in safety.

Norma looked at her and knew that she was not strong enough to withstand for any time the hurricane winds of scorn that would descend upon her if she were ever foolish enough to admit her inability to produce the earrings. She had been toying for some time with an idea. An idea so repugnant that she had been constantly attempting to thrust it from her mind. But her mind was in no state to put up a proper fight against it and the flimsy barricades she set up could no longer offer protection from its glittering assault. Her back was now being firmly pressed to the wall. Her vanity and her lust for social power were enough to impel her to take even the most desperate and distasteful measures. There was no more time. She had to make a decision.

"Next week." She said. "I goin' surprise you wit' them next week."

M ingy removed the huge grapefruit from the plate.

"You want some o' this?"

He was smiling, but Norma could see that he was nervous and still a little surprised. She remembered his discomfiture as he had responded to the uncertain knock at his door clad only in an old pair of white briefs. She smiled to herself as she recalled how he had searched in panic about the dingy one room house until he had located a pair of short khaki pants. Somewhere in her mind, too, burned disturbing memories of the sight of his thick, strong legs and the way in which the briefs had emphasised the outline of his male organs.

"T'anks." She said.

He held the fruit in both hands. He placed his two thumbs in the hole at the top of it. His biceps and pectorals bulged in a brief contraction. The grapefruit emitted a strange, sucking sound and split itself into two sections. He handed one to her and kept the other for himself.

"Somet'ing wrong? ... Miss B. all right?"

"My mother all right."

She watched with interest as he ate. First removing the thick, whitish membrane to reveal the succulent flesh of the fruit. Forgetting her presence and from force of habit he then used the very tip of his tongue to knock the pips from their resting places. A number of pink, puckered pockets glistened invitingly up at him. His preparations complete, he used both hands to hoist the fruit up to his head. His thick lips enveloped the mushy mass. His strong jaws moved up and down as he slowly sucked the sweet juice into his mouth.

"An' how you keepin'?" He wiped his mouth briefly with the back of his hand.

This was the time to tell him. This was her opportunity to blurt out the whole embarrassing situation. To offer to make the sacrifice she had decided to make and be done with it.

No. There had to be another way.

"Look. I goin' home. I don' know why I come up here. I sorry to bother you."

"Norms. You can't bother me."

She rose to leave.

"Hey!" He said with nervous gaiety. "You like you pierce you ears. You really gettin' special. You must show me the earrings when you put them in."

"I ain' get them yet." She said, hoping that he would begin to understand the situation.

He did. A little. "Well le' me buy them for you nuh." There was eagerness in his voice. "I would be glad."

She hesitated, waiting for him to continue; for him to demand what she was sure he would want to demand.

"Please." He said. "I would love to give you somet'ing to make up for .... You know wha' I talkin' 'bout."

She looked at him now and was surprised at what she was beginning to see and feel. He was old. He had to be at least forty years old. But she could still see an eager boy looking through those smiling eyes. She could somehow picture that same irresistible smile on the face of some mischievous ten year old Mingy begging for fruit or loose change. How could one so lovable be so unloved? The maternal urge began to stir within her.

"All right." She heard herself say. "But they have to be eighteen carat gol' otherwise they would rotten out my ears. An' real purty."

"You goin' like them. Don't worry."

"An' I have to have them before next Monday."

"Come to me Friday evening 'bout this same time. I will have them fo' you."

She peeked out the jalousies to make sure that no one was passing outside. "Goodnight, then." She said.

"Goodnight." There was soft regret in his voice. "Get home safe."

Her heart was light as she retraced the circuitous route she had taken to reach his house. She had developed a faultless databank of alternative combinations of gaps and alleyways through countless childhood games of hide and seek. She knew the entire village like the back of her hand and could quickly give the slip to anyone foolish enough to attempt to follow her.

◆ ◆ ◆

Mine is the prettiest
Do you hear my Sissy Oh!

Her next visit found him well prepared. There was fried chicken and cold soft drinks on the table. He was clean shaven. He had "showered" (in the backyard with an old wash pan and a "tot" with holes in the bottom) and was wearing clean clothes and an aftershave. Her attention did not dwell too long on these details. Her eyes groped wildly around the room for some sign of the life-saving earrings.

He noticed her anxiety and decided that he would

not prolong her suffering. He sprawled himself on the bed and fumbled around behind it for a short while. Finally, he grunted in satisfaction and got up.

"Here." He said and handed her a small package. His face bore that mischievous, boyish look that had endeared him to everyone in the village and was now beginning to impress her own heart.

She almost snatched the package from his hand and tore unashamedly at the bright wrapping paper. Finally she managed to open the box, revealing the polished beauty she so desired nestled in a soft white bed of contentment.

Mingy knew that he had done right. His face displayed even more happiness than hers. She gazed at her jewels and he at his, at the sparks of joy and gratitude radiating from her entire being.

"You want to put them on?"

She was afraid to touch them. She had never possessed anything so ... so abstract. She almost believed that they would suddenly explode into a puff of smoke and vanish with the wind.

"Le' me put them in for you then." He was beginning to lose some of his fear of her.

She did not resist as she felt his rough fingers gently slide the thorns from her earlobes. He reached from behind her and removed one of the

glistening ornaments from the box. Slowly, lovingly, he eased the thin hook through the small
opening. She felt no pain, only an expectant thrill
as the probing metal filled and expanded the snug
space that had been provided for it. Then his fingers flicked and bumped the inside of her ear as he
fumbled with the catch.

As he proceeded to insert the second earring
Norma began to become aware of his close presence behind her. His nearness seemed to envelop
her. She no longer felt the terror and disgust of
their earlier encounter. Her body was now responding with a wild and willing desire. His
deep breathing as he struggled with the annoying
catch. The smell of the after-shave lotion he had
over-splashed on his face. The heat emanating
from his hard, heavy body filled the small space
between them. It touched her and excited her. It
was all she could do to stop herself from sinking
insensible to the floor.

He managed to fasten the catch on the second
earring and swiftly retreated to the table in the
centre of the room.

"You want some chicken?" His voice was a deep,
disturbed growl.

She had begun to admire herself in the mirror.
Yes!....Yes! She could now parade. She could now
"pompousette" in front of Lolita Jordan and Shirley and all of her other small minded acquaint-

ances. Her coronation was but a few short hours away.

His eyes adored her from the bed where he sat with his plate of fried chicken.

"Some there for you when you ready, hear?"

She suddenly remembered something.

"I can't wear these home, though. You could take them out for me?"

Before he could answer she had dropped down on the bed beside him. He was surprised but he did not move away. She sat there, facing him and the pent-up desire once more forced itself to the forefront of his mind. He wiped his hands on a napkin and gently began to fumble with the delicate catches. He tried desperately to concentrate on her ears. To avoid looking into her eyes. But it was too much. The closeness of her. The look of intense concentration on her face. Her mouth half opened as she mentally followed the progress of his fingers on her earlobes.

 It was too much for him. Once again, his body broke free of all mental restraints. Once again, his head shot forward and his mouth descended to close itself over hers. This time though, there was no violent protest, no struggle to escape. To his surprise he felt a willing response, an acceptance in her soft lips. He could feel her push her body closer to his, feel her small arms attempting to encircle his muscular frame. He felt no elation only a profound gratitude as together they sank onto the welcoming bed.

N ew mun." Mrs. Pierre said and crossed herself.

"God bless me eyesight, to see the moon another night..." Norma's mother began.

"...An' increase me appetite." Her little brother completed the rhyme.

Everybody laughed.

"You got plenty mout' but ah hear you ain' doin' too good at school." Mrs. Pierre said sternly. "Here then, if you appetite increasing so." She held out an overripe mango.

Norma looked longingly at the suspended sliver of light. It signalled the approach of evening, her favourite time of day. Soon, very soon, somewhere amid the vines and bushes of the beach or on the lush savannah carpet he and she would join together to reach out to the heavens and this new moon. Sometime, before or after, or in between, their united spirits would soar in soft sleep high and happy above their love-locked bodies on the ground.

This was new. This devotion, this tenderness, was all so new that for the first few weeks of it she felt like an unworthy impostor. His constant attentions, however, soon forced her to accept and thrill to her new importance. He could only afford to offer her inexpensive things but she was always aware that the brightest diamond or flashiest automobile would be hers if he had the means of obtaining it. The physical sensations she so enjoyed were soon enhanced and intensified by the emergence and growth of a sincere devotion on her own part. This close association with him, this intimate knowledge of his soul, his un-affected charm, his ability to put any and every-one at ease. These things, and others more diffi-cult to identify, soon caused her to "fall in love" with him.

The love songs from the radio, the love stories in magazines, the love letters in the advice columns of newspapers now all became real to her. She identified only with the ones that bragged of new love and eternal commitment. The others, those sad tear-jerking ballads and hard luck tales caused her only a mild uneasiness that would disappear at the sight of his smile.

He missed no opportunity to remind her of his de-votion. "Listen carefully." He would say, with an air of almost comic seriousness. "I love you real bad, girl." She wanted to believe it. She did be-lieve it but she was afraid that any overconfidence on her part might offend some powerful watcher. So she would sometimes hang her head, or try to look away, but he would take hold of her chin between his thumb and forefinger. Gently, but firmly, he would turn her face until she was looking directly into his eyes.

"Never! We goin' never break up. You hear wha' I tell you?"

She felt herself to be vulnerable. The love she had allowed herself to feel for him had increased her happiness but reduced her self-sufficiency. He, in turn, sensed the beginning of this emotional dependence on him and became more relaxed, more confident in his dealings with her. Yes, he was happy. He would have been content with less, far less. A mercenary interest was all that he had expected to excite in her and he would have been willing to give his all for a few crumbs of feigned affection. Yet, here he was, with the whole delicious great-cake on his platter. He would be a fool not to try to enjoy it for a long, long time.

It lasted for three years. Then the doubts and second guesses knocked on their door and demanded satisfaction. Their happiness, their love, the mutual caring and respect had spread itself like a layer of strong mortar over the weak and uneven brickwork of their relationship. Now, as the tiny cracks began to open and spread, as the plaster began to flake off and drop all around them, they were forced to turn and reluctantly stare at the weak and shifting foundation on which they had based their eternal togetherness.

She was the problem. Her youth, her inexperience. Every morning her mirror would scream sense at her, demanding that she return to her original plan to find a man of worth. A man who would provide for her now and in the future. If she did not, it reasoned, she could find herself on her own fortieth birthday struggling to feed two or three little Mingies on his old age pension.

Her mother and her friends unaware of her attachment, also began to address her case. Their nagging advice did little to quell the turmoil in her soul. And as the barrage of questions and demands began to make her life at home unbearable, she decided that the time had come to put and end to the relationship.

The break, she knew, had to be clean and final. She had read enough love story magazines and advice column replies to know this. There must be no backsliding. No running to and from him until her love turned to frustration and her frustration to hate. She had to wait though, until the time was right. She knew that she lacked the strength to successfully withstand the withdrawal pains that would result. And so her mind probed and pondered between periods of doubt and ecstasy for some solution to present itself.

The Answer walked politely through their front house door. His clothes, she could tell, were purchased overseas. The cologne he was wearing wafted its unfamiliar but pleasant fragrance around them. He was tall, brown-skinned, and although his jacket and tie looked out of place in their poorly furnished front house, his good breeding made him appear to be right at home.

"Norma, this is Miss Sivers boy, Archie. Don' tell me you can' remember he."

She remembered him all right. As a child he used to stand outside their front window and tease her because she was not allowed to leave the house. He would call her a little monkey and make the most annoying faces. The happiest day of her young life was the day he and his family moved away.

"He workin' 'pon a boat now, you know." Her mother continued.

A *Seaman?..* With only one small ring on his finger? So slim ... and so conservatively dressed? She found it hard to believe. He soon removed her doubts, however, with animated, even boastful tales of his trips to places that she did not even know existed. He talked about Lisbon as if it were a bus trip away. He wowed her with tales about city buildings so tall a man had to "bend back" in order to view the top of them. He thrilled her with descriptions of clothes, jewellery and appliances. He made her shudder at the thought of eating fish and chips from newsprint or bread that had been transported under somebody's armpit.

After he had gone and she lay in bed, her mind

revisited its familiar world where Mingy's strong arms encircled and protected her, where his hard body and soft snores sent surges of hot breath and warm vibrations over her back. Tonight, though, visions of silk dresses and expensive restaurants tried to force themselves between them. They would disappear, only to return later, disrupting some sweet moment of imaginary bliss. She was like a person attempting to view two television channels at the same time. She could find no little knob at hand to control their transmissions and even if she could obtain one, she did not know which programme she should choose to watch.

Weeks passed and still she hesitated. Her tongue silenced by the beauty of Mingy's ready smile; overruled by the power of his lingering kisses. Everything about him now seemed more attractive, every moment spent in his company more precious. It was if her guardian angel or some other wise, invisible entity was silently urging her to stop and reconsider. To choose love.

Archie, encouraged by her mother, came to visit them more often now. She knew why. She was no fool. Men had been directing their attentions towards her since she was eleven and although he was shy and clumsy, especially for a Seaman, she was certain that he was trying to court her. He started bringing her gifts which she was pleased to accept. Her mother and friends beamed their knowing approval. He would make a good, acceptable boyfriend or ...... Husband! He would provide a good home and she would maintain it. Love was for young girls, a woman required security.

The time approached for his ship to return to sea and with it the moment when she would have to wrench her attention from romance to reality. In hesitant clichés and profuse promises Archie expressed his love and desire for her. She made her decision. She told him that she was willing to be his but her conscience forced her to beg for a delay. There was an important duty that she had to perform.

It was awful. The words she had so carefully chosen to soothe and reassure Mingy fell like big, grey boulders onto his stooped and silent frame. When she was finished he lied bravely; telling her that he could "see with her." He was willing to abide by her decision. Yet her heart could somehow hear him scream at her: "Please! Not yet. Not now."

She understood. She yearned to comply. Her mind too was screaming for it to stop. Their thoughts and emotions were by now enmeshed and interwoven like the tangle of love vine on a bush. It should require years of patient unwinding for them to be separated. The surgical slash of a tongue's sharp edge could do it, but at what cost? With the dry season approaching, their battered souls would slowly shrink to brittle skeletons and this sweet, sucking parasite would have long ago withered and fallen away.

And so they made their final offerings; wrote their last chapter of passion and joy. All the delights that he had reserved in secret store for her gradual gratification were tonight brought out and humbly laid before her. She had never before and she knew that never again would she be privileged to enjoy such total satisfaction. He poured the essence of his very being within her. He struggled to ensure that her body's departure would not serve to sever the spiritual links that so closely bound them.

There was no parting embrace. No fervent "God bless you" as she opened the door to go. He sat there silent on the bed, staring between his knees at some fascinating object down on the floor.

"Goodnight." She whispered, but he did not answer.

"Goodnight." She whispered again from the darkness outside ... and then slowly closed the door.

◆ ◆ ◆

It was with an effort that she managed to respond to Archie's attentions. It was pleasant though, to have an open relationship one that could bear the stamp of approval of her parents and peers. He introduced her to the cinema. He taught her to dance. He took her to "brams" and for long bus rides in the country. He was a man any woman would desire, charming, attentive and generous but he was not Mingy. In her dreams, whenever she was alone, even when her body was engaged in lovemaking sessions with Archie her memory would flood her mind with sweet and futile yearnings for the past.

The ship finally came and took Archie away. He promised that he would be back to her in a few months' time. She knew that she would not miss him. She never thought about him in his absence. He was a duty she had to perform, a consequence of her womanhood. This, she reasoned, was life where happiness was always incomplete, every choice imperfect. The wise decision was never practical and the practical decision never wise. He was her practical choice. She could not, like Mrs. Pierre, struggle through a life of hard work and uncertainty. She did not have the strength. She could not, like her mother suffer physical discomfort and neglect in the sweet cause of eternal love. She lacked the patience.

She was no fool. She realised that she was not a superior being so how could she overcome or escape the laws that directed the entire Universe - the duality that formed and governed every situation. She knew that to receive and to win, she must learn to lose and to sacrifice. She had no problem with this, but she feared the third factor. *Uncertainty.*

<blockquote>

Down Belly Mama
Down belly Mama
Down Belly, Mama belly
Swell like Cassava....

</blockquote>

When the disruptions of her body's normal functioning signalled the imminent arrival of a new player in the game she was filled with a welcoming joy. If Archie was as bland and traditional as he appeared to be this microscopic man within her should have no difficulty in binding him. She was now certain of that comfortable, clean home, imported clothes and a regular hairdo. She would have security. Her gamble was beginning to pay off.

She therefore shed with confidence the last vestiges of childhood and began the painful ascent up the nine stair-steps that would enable her to experience the ultimate glory of physical life. As she moved forward, the world stopped to note and comment on her progress. Some of the many men who had been denied the solicited opportunity to be partners in this great project pelted spit balls of venomous humour towards her inattentive ears. Some of her own sex briefly interrupted her evening walks with soft enquiries and kindly advice, reserving their jealous observations for future spiteful speculation. She, like a rose in a strong breeze swayed only slightly in the face of these in-effectual blasts. Her only defence was her breath-taking beauty; her only retort her radiant smile.

For there was new life within her, some sweet stranger that she cuddled and cooed at through the thick cover separating his world from hers. She yearned for the moment of their meeting, the chance to introduce him to the many mysteries of his new existence. His usefulness to her as a ball and chain no longer mattered. He had become a goal in himself, a source of life-giving sustenance in the arid future she had been forced to choose.

Mingy had reverted to his shadowy, rat-like exist-ence. Everybody knew that he was around but no-body ever knew where. Norma had not seen him since the night of their painful parting and this conscious effort on his part to keep away from her was helping her heart to heal. Her relation-ship with Archie, and now with the child within her had afforded her little time to brood. Her nights were often filled with pleasant dreams of their past happiness but she experienced no bit-terness nor regret. She was young, resilient. She possessed the power of her beauty and now there was this new security rolling and tumbling in her womb.

The letter dropped like a bomb from hell onto the shed roof floor. "Post!" Bernard shouted and tick-ticked his ginger squeezer rapidly away. There were only five shopping days to Christmas. He had no time to pause for a cool glass of lemonade or to impart a few humorous and suggestive observations on Norma's condition. He would make up for it on the big day when he and his posse would come with noise and mild curses to raid the larder and drink out the drinks.

Norma picked up the envelope. There was an English stamp on it. An unfamiliar hand had barely managed to scrawl her name and address on it. From Archie, she thought, and wondered for the first time why he had not written before. She hoped that the letter would say that he would soon be returning. She needed money for Christmas shopping and for baby clothes. She anxiously tore at the envelope until she had the folded sheet of paper in her hand. She gingerly unfolded it but no cleverly concealed pound notes came into view. She sucked her teeth in disappointment then lifted the letter to the light and began to read. "Dear Norma......" it began.

Her father's rage usually flared like a sudden brush fire. It would blacken their happiest moods and fill all around them with thick clouds of foul, monotonous epithets. It terrorised much but consumed little and burned and blustered only as long as it took her mother's quiet tears to put it out. Tonight was different. Tonight it was directed at Norma and its scathing scorn and vulgar accusations might have resulted in verbal or physical retaliation were she not indulging in her own self recrimination. His anger only served to strengthen her temporary self-loathing and the few snatches of his sermon that penetrated her consciousness often made her nod in involuntary agreement.

"*A marri'd man!* Marjorie you le' this li'l foolish bitch bring a marri'd man in here. A man wit' a big wife in Englan'. You le' he fool she off wit' a few cheap t'ings. You encourage he to …. Look! Look she there now full up wit' a li'l bad get bastard an' the fatha somewhere up in Englan' or in France tellin' he wife to write letters down here lambasin' she….. look! *it ain' landin' in here.* you hear me?...

She ain' bringin' no li'l bad get brute in here to eat up the food I have to work so hard for." His passion overflowed its banks. "Look she have to leave my house, you hear. *Try an' get she out o' my place.*"

Her mother tried to protest this decision. Her brother even broke his usual sullen silence to offer pleas on her behalf.

"Who don' like what I say can go 'long wit' she. All o' wunna can lef'. I don' care."

"The weak when oppressed must somehow shed their affliction. Their brittle moral structure can not for long withstand the weight of life. The hostility they show is not of their own making, they are but helpless pawns in the propagation of pain."

This observation, offered by Poodle to those outside the window caused shrieks of merriment to burst from the darkened crowd. They were, after all, part of this soap opera. They had a right to look on and entertain themselves. The best sport, they knew, was yet to come. Their aloof queen, their untouchable baby doll had now been daubed with a mark of shame so enduring that it could never be erased. It was a living disgrace that would probably exist longer than she existed. It would always be there, to confront and deny her every effort to regain her former exalted status. Their taunts and barbs, delivered at the worst moments would serve to keep her in line.

She would be aware of the rules. It was perfectly permissible for one to attempt to rise above the common level of smug ignorance and interpersonal abuse. No woman or man could, however, expect to attain these transcendent heights in possession of a good reputation for it would be the very first casualty in the struggle for self improvement.

Norma had to try to take stock of the situation. The secure existence she had so yearned for was now gone. The gamble she had made had not paid off. She could not at this time afford to gaze too deeply into the future. Her immediate needs would have to be taken care of. She had to find a house for herself and her child. That was her first priority. After that problem was solved she would face the other difficulties and overcome them.

Her mother tried to convince her that her father's words were words spoken in shocked anger and were not to be taken seriously. But she was wrong. He was deeply hurt. A daughter deflowered and disgraced is man's greatest source of pain. He could not bear to see his little girl reduced to this state but he had long ago been rendered incapable of expressing any emotion but anger. Every evening he would return from work to abuse Norma for delaying her departure until her mother was finally convinced of the seriousness of his demands. Norma had to go....but where? There were no relatives to take her in. No money to pay rent.

And so he came, shy and embarrassed to their front door. Norma's mother greeted him with effusive warmth for she loved him like a brother. She worried when she did not see him for long periods and worried even more to see him now. His eyes were red from liquor and lack of sleep; his face unshaven, teeth yellowed from lack of attention. He was leaving, he told them. He was returning to the country to help his family work their "groun'."

"I hear the girl lookin' for someplace to stay." He said. "So I thought that she could stan' in the house an' care it fo' me. Make sure it don' run to ruin, you know."

Her mother asked about the rent.

"Rent? Wha' rent?" He laughed. "I can't charge nothin' for that l'il place. I only here hopin' the two o' wunna don' get vex wit' me for insultin' she wit' it."

Norma lay listening on the easy chair. She forced herself to keep her head averted from him but she hung on to his every word. She listened and understood. *I love you real bad girl,* her trained ears were hearing. "I love you bad enough to gi' you my house an' lan'. An' anytime you want my life....you can take it." She had laughed happily the night he had said those words to her, but she was crying now.

She wanted to rush and embrace him but there was a bulging obstacle in the way. She had already sensed his eyes sadly surveying her burdened womb. The garden bed where he had expected to plant sweet flowers now infested with an alien and inextricable weed. She had to reach him somehow. Somehow try to lift his spirits and ease his pain. Her fingers reached up to fondle and caress the gold earrings he had given her so many years ago.

"T'anks," she said softly, " an' God bless you." She did not turn her face.

She hoped that he would somehow understand.

Her mind at last freed from the problem of providing shelter for herself and her little one she began the task of repairing the rents in the bond that had been formed between them. Archie's sins could not be allowed to mar this unique relationship. The child was her, too. A living bud from her body slowly separating in order to extend her existence and the existence of all those absent who had mixed and melded their features and characteristics to form the unique her. She was the flower; the major nurturing force. Archie, a mere bee who had wrought this wonder in clumsy pursuit of his own self satisfaction, buzzing off in greedy ignorance of his true purpose in life. She could never resent this child for to do so would be to curse her own existence. To neglect this new being would be to jeopardise her prospects of attaining immortality.

And so it was with patience and humility that she ascended the final stair-step. She lay herself down but could not rest until she had assisted her infant in completing the first and most important of the many labours he would have to perform during his stay. At last he slithered through the portal, screaming his lifelong need for comfort and warmth. She screamed, too, at first in agony but then in joy as she perceived his little countenance. There was no mistaking the resemblance, the beauty that transcended physical configurations. Thank God! Thank God! The seed of the usurper had not prevailed. Weeds could not take root in such unwilling soil. Only the sweet, soft flowers of Mingy the master gardener could flourish there. She had not lost. Their devotion would not die. For cradled in her arms was one who would serve to propagate their perfect blend of love throughout the world for spreading generations to come.

She had shelter. She had a beautiful being to love her. Now it was time for her pursuit of physical security to recommence. Her mother did what she could to assist with the infant. She often delivered fruits and ground provisions that a "good friend from the country" had brought for her. But Norma was unwilling to rely entirely on the assistance of those who loved her. She needed to be in a position to support herself, at least until she could meet the man she needed to protect her from the world.

Her mother had suggested that she take a job. She was ready to defy her husband and mind the baby during the day. But Norma knew what the jobs available to her would entail. It would mean deserting her own child for the entire day and well into the night so that other strange children could receive her attention. A job meant discarding her pride and her talents outside the gates of some "great house." A job meant submitting to the every whim of often cruel and pretentious people who were stupid enough to believe themselves superior to her because their skins lacked protection from the sun.

There were things she needed that her mother could not provide and she was not prepared to allow her child to suffer. Once again she was tempted to satisfy her needs by questionable means. Once again, she knew that there would be a terrible price to pay. For if she took the action she was contemplating she would destroy the close friendship she now shared with her mother. Mingy would recoil to the country and she would probably never see or hear of him again. She, however, was a mother now, responding to the same strong natural forces that motivated the females of almost every species on the planet. She knew what she believed she had to do and she did it without qualm. At first with fear and distaste but eventually with shameless defiance.

Soon the word spread rapidly from man to man. A new outlet had just opened and the goods were very good.

The child stirred and yawned. Something was disturbing his afternoon nap. A sound. The sound it seemed of rain dripping into a pool of water. Splish......Splish. It reminded him too of the sound he made as he sucked on an ackee or dunk seed, squeezing it hard between his tongue and fat jaws and then releasing the pressure on it. Squish.....Squish. He was half awake now. He could feel that the bed was moving beneath him, bouncing up and down. He tried to raise himself on one elbow but his little body resisted his efforts. It needed rest so that it could continue to build and grow. His eyes would not focus properly. They were cemented together by some itchy substance. He rubbed them open and stared.

He had grown accustomed to seeing men come to their home. Some of them were friendly men, patting his head, poking his tummy and pulling at his little arms and feet. Others ignored him and spoke roughly to his mother who often responded with loud, angry words that he did not understand. This man was new. This man was different. His skin was pale and polka dotted with random red blotches; his hair was like a woman's hair but shorter. The men before him smelled of rum and sweat and tobacco. He smelled of perfume.

What was this man doing in their bed? What

were they up to? It did not make sense to him ... the constant moving up and down; the grunts, the heavy breathing. It was not a game, he could tell. His mother was not tickling and teasing the man as she usually did with him. She was not laughing or growling in mock ferocity. Her face bore a patient, resigned expression. The man, too, appeared tense and uncertain. The child watched some more, hoping to witness some interesting development, but the action continued bland and monotonous as before. His eyelids became heavy again. His body screamed for rest. Slowly his head descended to the pillow.

He awoke later to find that they had gone and he was alone again. He was a calm and self-sufficient youngster. He would content himself with his toys and the sweet sounds and invisible voices that came to him from the box some man had hung upon their wall. His mother would be back by evening. She had to. If she did not return before the sun disappeared and darkness shut off his view of the world fear would claim him. She would come back to find him huddled and weeping in some corner of the house. In the days that followed she would try to amend her ways, to shower him with love and attention. But soon, too soon again, she would forget, or be forced to forget and the awful fear of abandonment would once more invade his being.

Now the sun was shining hot and hearty through

the open window. He rolled over lazily. The bed was wet and warm in the place his mother and the strange man had recently occupied. His bottle had somehow been knocked to the foot of the bed. He crawled over to get it. A money fly hastened from the sticky nipple as he approached. The child lifted the bottle, popped it into his mouth and sucked reflectively. The milk was cold and slightly sour but he drank it anyway. Sometimes there had been no milk at all and he had been forced to suck and suck on the unyielding nipple until burning hunger made him shout his complaints to the uncaring room.

He finished the bottle and let it roll away from his mouth, down over his chubby chest and arms, onto the bed. A shiny object jumped and clinked as the bottle passed over it. A coin. It must have fallen from the strange man's pocket. He crawled over to it and picked it up. It was shiny, but it was hard and cold. It could not engage his interest for very long. Something else from the man's pocket now gleamed flat and glossy on the bed. This object was pretty. There was a picture of a huge boat on it. It was smooth and soft to the touch. He grabbed it eagerly.

It did not take him long to pry open the cover and expose two neat rows of mysterious black-tipped objects. He chortled in delight. New toys! He played all sorts of games with them that afternoon. He ripped them gleefully from the box.

He stuck them in his mouth and his ears. He scraped the black sulphur off the cardboard sticks and chewed them up. He tossed them about and hunted them down. He rubbed them together. He rubbed them all over the box....

Then the magic began. The sudden spark of fire filled him with delight. He watched fascinated as the flame burned its hot bright path along the length of the small stick. It reached the end now. He felt a sharp pain as it made contact with his fingers. He dropped it quickly but did not cry. There was too much to see, too much to enjoy. The pee-stained bedclothes now burst into a larger flame. The beauty of the fire claimed his full attention. He could not avert his eyes from its crackling vitality. He watched it spread and spread along the bed hissing and popping in its own excitement. He yearned to watch it forever but it was now becoming too much for him. His eyes were finding it difficult to withstand the strain of observing its brilliance. He fought to keep them open, to prolong the joy he felt in the presence of this glorious phenomenon. It was too much. His eyelids came together and resisted his efforts to force them apart. He fell once again into a deep, deep sleep.

It's Murder! It's Murder.....

Norma was happy. Hank had been very pleased, very generous. He had even introduced and recommended her to Jerry. This cruise ship visit was a wonderful opportunity for her. With luck she could make a killing tonight. She had one regret. The child would be alone and hungry again. She would not be able to get away. She had to make the most of the moment. He was growing. Maybe soon he would be able to take care of himself.

"Hey, Baby, why so quiet? Here, have another drink." Jerry placed his hand possessively on her naked leg. It felt clammy and hot.

She sipped the rum and coke and smiled up at him. A professional, calculating smile. She could see that this Jerry had a weak head. He would be quick and easy. A real pushover....

But then the sudden sirens of misfortune that had screamed denial of so much happiness and hope screamed again for her. The rushing feet, the peeping eyes, the malicious tongues that broadcast the insensitivity of darkened and humiliated souls now once more mocked and laughed at her.

They had her again and would give her no quarter as she ran barefoot and bawling to the scene. No one would answer her enquiries. The ingrained contempt they felt for her suppressed any pangs of sympathy. Even the pain they could clearly read in her sunken eyes did not move them. Unclean. She was unclean. They could not be seen to touch her for fear that their own blemishes might be somehow revealed.

She reached the spot. Her terrified eyes probed the scene. Something lay charred and smoldering in the corner where the bed used to be. She looked hard and seemed to distinguish a blackened head, a few cracked bones. Purified. Somehow the word drummed into her ears. Purified. Her little Mingy, a spirit fashioned in the purest fires of true love. A gift too precious for one so unworthy to nurture and sustain. Purified. His beauty could no longer be tarnished by her example and neglect. A spirit so precious could not be allowed to be lost or destroyed. And so he had been purified, purified and reclaimed. Maybe the pain of this parting would somehow redirect her steps; maybe someday she might be invested with another valuable trust.

Why, oh! Why, she wondered, did she always have to suffer so. What curse, what Obeah had been dumped on her to limit and destroy her every opportunity for love and fulfillment? It was too much! Her spirit rebelled. Her mind was over-heating inside of her. Her body too, felt hot, so hot she could almost experience the sheer agony that had tormented the flesh and spirit of her uncomprehending child. Smoke seemed to fill her mouth and throat, suffocating her. Her clothes became hot, tight bands of metal, constricting her body, burning into her flesh. She began to thrash about; screaming, pleading, cursing incoherently in languages even she did not understand. Unmindful of the shocked silence or amused titters of those in the crowd she tore wildly at her clothes, struggling in a frenzy to liberate herself from the evil that was attempting to smother her. Then, a sudden, sharp, pain shot through her body ending her frenzy, forcing her back to the world in which she presently existed.

The shock wore off and gave way to an acceptance of reality. He was gone. All the little love in her life was now gone. No one would assist or comfort her now. She was to blame. She knew that she had to accept the responsibility for that state of affairs. She had been forced by her choice of profession to isolate herself from others. She was not one to accept a position of inferiority in society. If she were not accepted as an equal she would contrive an air of false superiority. She could be friendly but never humble. To patronise or otherwise offend her was to risk the sharp edge of her abusive tongue. And so, in these last few years, she had been forced to live like some cornered animal: defiant and aggressive but fearful and anxious to escape.

She looked into her hand now and saw the reason for her physical discomfort. Her frenzied clutching had somehow ripped one of the earrings through the tender flesh of her ear lobes. It glinted at her like some huge golden ship grounded in a crimson lake. Her mind told her that it was a hopeful omen. A promise that her sore and smarting wounds would someday heal.

◆ ◆ ◆

Johnny wash he shirt in a tot
Johnny hang it on a flat rock
Suzie went to see if it dry
Johnny cuff she in she left eye
Johnny one .. Suzie two
Johnny ....

WHUP!　　The blow struck with a dull, heavy force. Norma felt the pain without surprise. The world to her was now a place where anything could happen. She welcomed every misfortune in the hope that she would soon satisfy her quota. WHUP! she felt the pain again but did not respond. Who was this stranger anyway? Why was he attacking her? Where had he been recently? Did he not see her hounded eyes on the front page of every newspaper? Heard her story on the evening news?

It was too soon for this. She had only just been released from the hospital where she had lain for weeks without thought or feeling. She had received no visitors, except the group of Christian youngsters who roamed the halls at visiting time offering hope, and encouragement in their prayers. Slowly, her soul had begun to assimilate this nourishment and the clouds of despair began to lift. Her physical strength returned and her empty mind began to function. She accepted that she would never be the contented housewife she had planned to be nor the rich old whore she had expected to be. She had no idea what her final destiny would be but she realised one thing. Life was full of twists and surprises. It was like a sweet stream taking everyone to his allocated destination. Those strong swimmers bold enough to defy the current would be forced eventually to thrash about in unhappy immobility until frustrated and exhausted, they decided to yield to the wisdom of the resistless tide.

"Free up! Free up!" The man hissed and hit her again. This time it really hurt. It was vicious enough to force the very food from her stomach. She choked as she struggled for control. A cry of pain at last escaped her lips.

A figure appeared in the doorway of the rum

shop across the road. It peered in their direction. "Beeserk. That is you out there?"

Beeserk! She remembered the name now from childhood tales of his numerous, inexplicable exploits. Beeserk would cut or chop anybody for the price of a drink. Beeserk would expose himself or publicly masturbate for a cigarette. Beeserk was an outpatient of the mental hospital. He often missed his scheduled treatments because he seemed to delight in tossing the attendants about whenever they came for him.

"Come!" He said and tried to drag her into the bushes beside the road.

"Beeserk!" The young man came out of the shop and began to cross the road . "Wha' it is you doin' out there?"

"Malicious bitch!" Beeserk hissed.

Relief flowed through Norma as the familiar figure approached them. Her little brother was a sturdy teenager now. She felt pride and joy at seeing him again. He stopped. He could see them clearly. Then he sucked his teeth.

"Wait, Beeserk. You mean she ain' even get out o' the horspital good an' gone back doin' tha' a'ready?" He sucked his teeth again and turned to walk back into the shop.

Mental instability can generate great physical

strength, they say. But so does fear, and love, and shame. Somehow or other Norma found the strength within her to tear herself away from her tormentor. She ran crying and pleading after her brother's departing figure but he ignored her. He re-entered the shop and she followed. Still pleading, still crying. Until the futility finally enveloped her. She was ready. To die. To blow away. She offered her unconditional and total surrender to whoever or whatever had been tormenting her for so long. She sat down and allowed her once proud head to sink submissively until it landed on one of the rum-stained tabletops.

When she finally looked up it was morning. Somebody was holding a cup of tea in front of her.

"Smoody, Smoody. I sorry." She said. Somehow he had managed to get her into bed. She noticed the brown spots where he had painted iodine on the bruises on her arms.

He brought some eggs and although she was almost too depressed to eat she found it impossible to refuse the humble, apologetic manner in which he offered them to her. Then, without quite knowing why she was doing it, she poured all the sad years of her womanhood over him. He sat and listened. He did not interrupt. He did not advise. He just sat, like a priest at confession while she leeched herself of the putrid waste that had been her past life.

"Would you like to stay here?" He asked when she was finished.

"But the people would talk." She protested. "I will only bring trouble for you."

"Do you have someplace else to go?

"No. ... But I don' want to put you in no trouble, Smoody. You know what people goin' t'ink now? You know wha' they goin' say?"

"Listen carefully." Oh! Why did he have to say those *words?* "The worst things people can say about me have already been said." He smiled with irresistible sincerity. "Besides. I going work you so hard you might 'buse me worse than anybody else."

That was ten years ago. In all those days she cleaned and cooked and washed and slept. In the evenings she served the drinks and joined in the dominoes, the cards and the gossip. Slowly, very slowly, they learned to accept her; and then to love her, though no one would admit it to her face. She felt herself being converted, through Smoody's soft influence into a generous and considerate woman. Warm, loving and .... happy. Maybe at last, she had found her Security.

Yet sometimes in the late night, amid the loud music and the free flow of refined rum and coarse conversation, some strange man would look askance at her now renovated body and tickle the palm of her hand as she made change. When this happened, horrifying images of lumps of smouldering charcoal would flash before her. Sweet arms that once tightly hugged her neck would turn before her mind's eye to charred and blackened bones. Then she would startle them all with loud screams and run in fear and sorrow back to her darkened room.

EPILOGUE

"Wait! Wha' happen? I hear they had a shootin' in here." Cleota rushed into the Hideaway looking out of place in her church clothes: The stiff, blue nylon dress and matching high-heeled shoes. The black painted Panama hat. She fanned herself with a cracked white handbag. Pink powder and perspiration formed lumps and puddles on her face.

"Man ... Cleota! You mean you mus' be in church an' chapel too? ... crown tha' man. I don' want my king to ketch col'." Clairmonte was trying to divide his attention between Cleota and the man on the other side of the draughts board. "The Father know you missin'?"

Cleota ignored him. She rushed over to Cynthia. Cynthia would know and Cynthia would be pleased to tell.

"An' where Congo get the gun from?" She asked at last.

"That is none o' you blasted business, woman." Congo's voice startled them. His head was still resting on the tabletop. They had all assumed that he was still asleep.

"Sorry, sir." Cleota said with mock civility. At another time she would have rebuked Congo but tonight she was in a happy and expansive mood. Her soul had been touched; her mind purged of all tension and hostility.

She had just been blessed to experience two hours of beautiful fellowship. First the familiar gospel choruses sung over and over with hypnotic regularity transporting all within the church to a state of mindless rapture. Heads rocking gently from side to side. Eyes accustomed to recording harsh reality for this moment rendered dazed and useless. Only tongues were necessary. Tongues to make loud and joyful noises. Tongues to intermittently mutter soft and gentle praises....."Dear Jesus....Sweet Jesus.." Only hearts were required, full and bursting with fervour and commitment. And hands, moving from side to side like slow windshield wipers .... Testifying ... Testifying .... Hips to twitch in spasms of sudden ecstasy ... And feet to stomp and crush the world's heavy burdens cast down by the power of grace from now enlightened heads and shoulders.

Then the sermon. Loud and passionate, interrupted only by shouts of agreement...."HALLELUJAH!" ..."PRAISE THE LORD!"

The pastor in the middle of his delivery paused to run swiftly and gleefully three times around the pulpit area. He had recently been involved in an automobile accident. His back had been injured. He had experienced difficulty in moving around. But his recovery had been swift. Very swift. Almost miraculous. "PRAISE THE LORD!" On regaining the rostrum he proceeded to shake his head and shoulders about with a vigour that was painful to watch, smiling and praising God.

Then, Esmeralda proceeded to trill in some eerie, ancient tongue words that seemed to speak of suffering, of passion and of ...Comfort. She stood there, before the altar, eyes closed, right hand raised aloft and made her unintelligible pronouncements. Not an "Amen" or "Hallelujah" could be heard throughout her presentation and hushed silence reigned for a long moment after she had ceased to speak.

It was a wonderful service. Cleota left the church happily relieved of all the "botherations" heaped upon her by her "Missee" and her Man ... relieved of everything except her curiosity. So, when she heard that gunshots had been "let go" in the Hideaway she felt constrained to go out of her way to properly investigate the matter.

She now regarded Congo's woolly head as it once more snored on the card table. He was indeed lucky that she was a Christian lady or he would have long ago felt the full weight of her tongue. Unlike the others, she did not fear him. She despised him. To her he was a traitor to his gender and to his race. No able-bodied Black man, especially as fine a specimen as he was, should

permit himself to be used as a lap dog and a convenience by a bunch of worthless foreign women.
She feared that it would spread. That future generations of young men would choose to follow
his disgusting example. If that happened, the day
would come when simple, God-fearing women
like herself would be without good men to comfort them.

"Cleota...You in here very long. You backslidin' or
wha'? Come an' fire one o' these, do." Clairmonte
brandished a "pint 'n' a half" bottle of white rum
and a glass. His wide, teasing smile anticipating
an angry response.

Cleota sucked her teeth. "Let me get out o' here."
She said in a superior tone. "Before I sin my precious soul." But she knew that there was nothing
she could say or do that would faze the fun loving
Clairmonte.

"If you don' sin it now you goin' be sure to sin it
when you get home. I pass and see Fordie bareback
at the window looking up the road in a certain
kind o' way. Very anxious ....." The men laughed.
"Very sharky! You may be in the spirit now chil'
but Fordie down there plannin' to get in the flesh."

CLAIRMONTE! .. Shut you foolish mout', do. I is a
Christian lady. You can't talk them t'ings to me."
Cleota rushed through the door.

"You min' she." Clairmonte could be heard to say.

"She like it even if it cook up in rice." Everybody laughed.

"Goodnight everybody." There was a hint of a giggle in Cleota's departing voice. ... "Hey! Where Poodle tonight?"

"He somewhere outside there. I t'ink he talkin' to a tree."

"Well if he ain' mad they ain' got none in Jenkins." Cleota muttered to herself as she walked briskly down the road. She was now anxious to get home. Clairmonte's earthy comments and observations had served to whet her appetite for whatever further fulfilment this exciting evening might have to offer.

❖ ❖ ❖

In the dark, holy hush beneath the trees Poodle discovered that thoughts, questions and inspiration would spring to his mind, and words issue from his lips with no conscious effort on his part. Here, away from the rum induced gaiety and vexations of the Hideaway he could recommit himself to the search for truth. For a purpose. Answers often came. Sometimes, in the frantic scurry of small crabs; in the faint whispers of vibrating leaves or in the warning hum of approaching raindrops.

Tonight it was the jarring contact of his back tooth with the hard casing of a tamarind seed that sparked his further enlightenment. After his tooth had unsuccessfully, and painfully, attempted to crush the object he had removed the seed from his mouth. He regarded it for a moment then began to ponder the fact that he held in his small hand the beginning of a huge and mighty tree. He looked up at the branches above him. In this tree were hundreds of fruit ... thousands of seeds. The potential for millions of new plants to spring up and continue.

 He knew, of course, that this would not happen. The majority of seeds produced by this and almost every other tree would not be allowed to germinate. They would be discarded ... just as he, himself would have been discarded had he not been the winner of that first race, that first titanic struggle against millions of his brothers and sisters. He had been forced to dance his way to victory. His little tail had twitched and shaken until it had propelled him to the point where he, and he alone, could grasp and claim the fabulous door prize ... a one-way ticket to this thing called LIFE. But why had he, he wondered, a humble half drunk fisherman, been awarded this rare opportunity when there no doubt existed among the discarded millions potential philosophers and healers of men?

Whatever the reason, he had been the chosen one. A seemingly insignificant speck nurtured and protected in a warm, dark womb and delivered, at the appointed moment into the cold light of limited self awareness. He could no longer suck directly from the walls of his new womb as he did in the old. He was now catapulted into an even more bitter and murderous competition with his brothers and sisters. He would have to suffer to survive here and he would in turn cause suffering. Humans, plants and animals he would somehow be compelled to injure and destroy. Surely there must be a better way. To murder and devour other living creatures was expressly forbidden yet it was done instinctively to survive. Oh! how he wished he had the capacity, like the trees, to drink from the Earth and eat from the Sun.

What was the unseen objective this time? He wondered. Were the millions on this planet rushing again to reach the portal to some new competitive existence or was this the Main Event .... the final elimination.

How many? How many would be chosen this time ... how many discarded? What criteria would be used to decide the winners? Would it be the acquisition of wealth? ... the ruthless scramble to "own" vast quantities of the Earth's components? Would it be Intelligence .... in whose name so much evil had been excused and so much suffering inflicted?

In the old womb everyone knew what was expected. Everyone swam in the same direction. This new womb was so complicated ... so full of choices; of conflicting and contradictory signals. How could one avoid being discarded like an unwanted tamarind seed? He sat fearfully silent for a moment. Then the truth of the old saying engulfed him: *"Let your Conscience be your Guide."*

So there WAS guidance. There WAS direction. There had also to be a purpose.

A breeze now shook the tree above him. A large, dry tamarind dropped from an overhanging bough and landed in his lap. He looked at it. The top of the shell had broken off on impact to reveal the first succulent segment. It peeped suggestively at him, like the exposed tip of a circumcised penis.

 He felt the stinging pain of the blow in his crotch and in his bowels and understood. He had been delinquent. He had not been playing his part. He had blindly and zealously swam his way into this world only to slam the door on others waiting to follow him. While his brothers and sisters were gleefully multiplying and replenishing the length and breadth of the island he only sat and questioned. He sought answers before he would summon another into this world. He demanded guarantees that the brutality of this earthly competition would not cause his flesh and blood to suffer here, and in the hereafter. But, in trying to spare them sorrow he had heaped it upon himself. In trying to protect them from the pain of the contest he had been denying them the glory of a possible Victory.

He picked up the long, knobbly tamarind pod and looked at it again. THEY ALWAYS BORE FRUIT. He had often seen bushes spring up in the scorching, unrelenting heat of the dry season. *Always* before they withered. *Always* before they succumbed. *Always* ... there would spring from their stunted branches next year's seeds ... next year's hope. He could take a hint. It was time for him to create the next link in his own chain.

He turned to leave. He paused. Somehow his movements at this time seemed impertinent and out of place. His deep reverie had blinded his senses to the unusual stillness that had gripped the land. The moon had long ago retreated behind a mass of dark cloud. The leaves and limbs of the high trees now drooped like tired shoulders. No breezes teased the bush and grasses. No lovesick crickets chirped their need. Somewhere ... Somewhere near ... the battle was being fought... Again.

"I want my change!" Congo said.

"Oh! God! You wit' that again. I t'ought you did forget 'bout that every sence."

"Wunna ain' hear I ain' leavin' here wit'out it. You t'ink I did makin' sport?"

Congo raised his head and upper body from the table. He had by now slept off the rum and other alcoholic concoctions that had been controlling his thoughts and actions. His aversion to being tricked and humiliated was not so easily dissipated. Now that he was sober, his righteous indignation was even more sharply focused, more easily translated into violence.

Immediately a silence, a bad silence, claimed the room. It was as if there was a bad taste in every mouth, a bad smell in every nostril. Everybody wanted to leave but nobody dared approach the door. They knew that anybody who ventured in that direction would be deemed the culprit and be punished accordingly.

Clairmonte sighed loudly. Something had to be done before this "noise" spoiled his entire evening's fun.

"Congo ... Congo ... It was me, Man." He lied. "I take up the four dollars."

"I had a feelin' it was you. Try and let me see them."

"I don' have four dollars 'pon me now. I goin' have to pay you later. You comin' in here tommor' night?"

"I want my money NOW. I ain' leavin' here tonight wit'out it."

Clairmonte had been hoping to defuse the situation but it seemed that he had only increased the power of Congo's imminent explosion. His wit and charm had eased him out of dangerous situations before. He had to rely on them to save him now.

He smiled. Even white teeth, shiny, broad, black forehead, healthy clear eyes, all emanating joy and light ...

"Man ... Congo ...."

"Don' skin you teets at me!"

Congo's hand rose and fell. The "pint 'n' a half" bottle shattered itself against the card table, spraying shards and tinkling fragments about the room. Only its long, jagged neck remained, twitching greedily in Congo's right hand.

"Man ... Congo ..."

"I TELL YOU HUSH!"

"Anger can turn a man into a devil, Smoody, and he forgets all that he was so painfully taught. He only feels the frenzied urge to strike out. To hurt. To "mash up". To kill! To free himself it seems from what he has become. To tread again the jungle of his birth ...."

The weapon rose high, fell swiftly and came up red. Nobody screamed. Nobody moved.

"Oh God! Congo." Clairmonte groaned. "You goin' kill me?"

The weapon rose again. And fell again. Clairmonte bucked and moaned like a woman at the height of passionate intercourse ... or rape.

"Oh God! ... Congo ... Oh God!..."

Smoody had been trying all this time to intervene but his body would not respond to his brain's urgent commands. His tongue somehow refused to address the raging Congo. His feet would not agree to transport his body to the area of conflict. "Wait." Something seemed to be saying to him. "Wait! Let me see what he is going to do."

The struggle to rise, to speak, to intervene was taking its toll of him. It was as through a daze that he saw the bottle neck rise and fall, saw the blood spurt into the air and drip-drop on to the floor. At this sight the Beast within him jumped and romped in ecstasy. It was useless. He could restrain it no longer. He now felt it rise and bound, almost tearing his heart asunder as it flew away from his confining goodness to the welcoming recesses of Congo's shattered soul. The strain of battle overcame Smoody. His senses were starting to shut themselves off. Then, he heard Norma's voice, shrill and desperate in the shocked and silent room.

"NO! TONY ... NO!"

She rushed between them, braving the blind, mechanical stabs and thrusts of his weapon. She tried to grasp him but sensed that it would take more than physical power to stay his hand. He had, at this point lost control of his actions. It was her responsibility now to save him.

This had been the first great gift with which she had been entrusted and here, too, she had failed. She had allowed it to be tarnished and corrupted and now almost destroyed. This was her last chance for redemption. This giant had a great soul that is why people feared and respected him That is why they insulted and brutalised him. She had to somehow establish contact with that powerful psyche and assist it in defying the perverted and destructive forces that were now in control. She therefore rushed between them. Ignoring the danger to her own being. Ignoring the searing assault of the broken glass as it gouged and cleaved the flesh from her arm.

Now, here, close to his familiar vibrations, she felt her entire being swell and overflow with the motherly love she had once freely and fearlessly lavished on him. Years ago. Before the drought. She tried to look into his eyes but she could not find them. Only the bloodshot glare of the Beast assailed her.

Congo's hand rose high and she half stooped, half crouched, her bent back fearfully and perhaps gratefully awaiting what could be the final thrust. But this time the hand did not fall. Somewhere in the big man's consciousness faint memories began to shake themselves awake. Memories of the days she fed and cleaned him. When she kept him safe from the big, bad boys in the daytime and the huffs and puffs of the big, bad wolf at night. When her promises of sweeties and sugarplums dried his tears. When her soft words and gentle kisses healed the bruises that would so often appear on his body.

      "NO! TONY ...NO! ...."

"Sis ...." The weapon clinked and clattered on the floor.

She took his hand, led him to a bench in the corner and gently sat him down. Slowly, lovingly, she smoothed his knotted hair and tidied his collar whispering long unspoken endearments and words of resurrected love. For the first time in many years his big head sank again onto her bosom. Then it happened.

Rumbling like thunder from deep within him; hissing and gushing in torrents from his eyes, from his very soul the pent-up pain and passion came. Norma's heart began to sing with joy. She knew that the brown days were over. The rains had come ... *at last!*

Arnold F Ward *is a prize winning author who has won several international awards for his writing. He is also an actor and playwright. He is a graduate of York University in Toronto and resides on the beautiful island of Barbados, West Indies.*

Arnold has appeared in several amateur theatre productions. He wrote and produced "The Stinger" and "Kaiso Queen" for the Barbados Landship Association, and directed the self-penned musical "Patsy".

Arnold was the frisky Frank in the popular television sitcom "Keeping up with the Joneses" and performed in the film "Sweetbottom".

Arnold's work may be purchased and reviewed at: https://www.amazon.com/author/arnie_ward.dear_aunt.knock

OTHER BOOKS BY THIS AUTHOR

DEAR AUNT

SISTER SPENCER (Part Two of the Dear Aunt Trilogy)

NDYUKA MAN (Part Three of the Dear Aunt Trilogy)

BAJAN LOVE

CHRYSALIS

GREATEST HITS

TWO BOATS: How West Indian Workers Helped NASA to Put A Man On The Moon

WHAT READERS SAY:

"Commending this Barbadian author for the enclosed passionate portrayals of the Barbadian experience and recognizing this novel as an appealing and exciting read .." **NATIONAL CULTURAL FOUNDATION, BARBADOS on Knock And Wait.**

"The use of language is very descriptive as well as the sentence construction. His use of metaphors was amusing and entertaining." Beverly Best on Knock And Wait.

"I really loved this book. Great reading. The kind of book that you curl up and read on a rainy day" B Angela Clarke on Dear Aunt

"Captivating .. There is excellent use of languauge." Beverly Best on Ndyuka Man.

*"Every story is a triumph of narration that transports the reader to the time and place and elicits an almost mystical identification with the central character."..***EDUCATOR reviewing Greatest Hits on Amazon.**

[The author] ..."shows compassion and understanding in his presentation of women – he knows them well"...Prominent Journalist Carolle Bourne of the **NATION** *newspaper reviewing "Bajan Love" on January 31, 1993.*

NDYUKA MAN

Part Three of The Dear Aunt Trilogy

Arnold Ward

Chapter 1: Leaving

People seldom accept good advice especially if it comes from a mother.

Edna knew this. She pulled at the collar of his shirt and brushed an invisible something from his shoulder.

"You sure that you still want to go?"

He did not want to go but he felt that he had no choice. There was no work. There was no hope.

"You can wait a lil longer. Trust in the Lord, Son. You goin' soon get somet'ing to do." The fear; the despondency in her voice. Here was her only son about to play a game of Yankee roulette and she could do nothing to stop him.

"Suppose you get kill?" In desperation she uttered again the dark thought that they had, for the past few weeks kept hidden in their souls. "Every week the postman does come to somebody in the village with

one of them black and brown letters."

Water shone from her big eyes and dripped onto her cheek. She dabbed at them with a balled up handkerchief.

"I can't live offa you and Dada forever," Courcey meekly protested. "I goin' only be gone for five years. I soon comin' back."

He looked at Boysie for support. His father had been quiet all this time. Standing there, wishing that the situation would go away. His usually smiling face was drawn. Deep wrinkles gouged his forehead. The awful dread in his heart was like the pain of a thrusting sword. He met his beloved son's enquiring eyes and slowly bowed his head. He understood Courcey's manly pride but that is all about the situation that he could accept.

Courcey looked across the pier at the hundreds gathered at the wharfside. The latest in a seemingly endless procession of sacrificial lambs. Many of the men were bedecked in their church suits, highly polished black shoes and felt hats. Their women, were also colourfully dressed for this sad, but hopeful occasion. Mothers, like Edna, were there, fussing over and cajoling their sons. Wives, girlfriends, fathers, brothers, children all creating a confusing cacophony. Many of them had come from the country districts, rising early to catch the bus where buses were available. Others rode on donkey carts or even walked for miles and miles to ensure that they were present to see their loved ones off. Over in one corner a group from an evangelical church was singing gospel choruses. One of their own was about to leave them. The preacher, with Bible in his right hand swung his left in time with the music.

Out over the bay the lighter men rowed their craft to and from the docks, each time loading and transporting a number of workers to the ship. Courcey could see a few boats leave the vessel and begin the return journey. A feeling of dread filled his being. Soon it would be his time to leave. The realisation that in a few short moments he would be severed from all that was familiar to him numbed his soul.

He had not been aware that his mother had been talking to him all this time. "And don't forget to write." He now heard her say.

A boat sidled up to the dock close by.

"Come, Courcey, man! Let we catch this one." Rat Trap shouted. He jumped into the boat and sat down, placing his battered, cardboard suitcase next to him to reserve the spot for Courcey.

"Comin'!" Courcey shouted back.

Boysie leaned forward to shake Courcey's hand. "Travel safely, son," he said hoarsely. He patted him on the back then hurriedly pulled away. Edna hugged her son tightly for a long moment. He could feel her stout body shake as she fought to control the sorrow that threatened to overwhelm her.

"Don't forget to write, hear Courcey. Don't forget to write. Let we know how you doing."

"I goin' write, Ma. I goin' write."

There were tears in his eyes and he could hardly see to make his way down to the boat. One of the lightermen held his arm and guided his stumbling steps along the gently rocking boat. He settled down on the seat beside Rat Trap and another passenger sat down beside him.

Soon they were pushing off from the dock. Courcey looked over his shoulder at the quay to see people waving, shouting and crying. Edna had collapsed in Boysie's arms, her entire body convulsing against him. A wave of shame swept over Courcey at the thought of the pain that he was causing the two people he loved most. Maybe he had been hasty in his decision to leave the island. Maybe, as Edna had said he could have used his skills as an artisan to make a reasonably comfortable life for himself. Jewel. She was the reason for his departure. He felt compelled to accumulate some money, to make himself a man of worth, in the hope that her father would accept him as an eligible suitor. But what about Jewel herself? She had never verbally committed to him and he was gambling his life and his family's happiness on what might have been to her a brief moment of weakness. He expected that by now she would have seen his letter. He could only hope that she indeed cared for him and would wait five years for his return.

The lightermen grunted as they swiftly pulled the oars and the boat lunged eagerly across the bay. Courcey continued to look through blurred eyes as his past and the loving island family on the dock slowly receded. He watched it growing smaller and more indistinct with each stroke. Then, the frantic pace of the oars slackened and they slid alongside the waiting ship. All eyes stared up, as so many had done before them at the murky and uncertain future that loomed grey and rusty above.